OPERATION VALENTINE

OPERATION ROMANCE BOOK 2

ELIZABETH MADDREY

Scripture quoted by permission. Quotations designated (NIV) are from THE HOLY BIBLE: NEW INTERNATIONAL VERSION®. NIV®. Copyright © 1973, 1978, 1984 by Biblica. All rights reserved worldwide.

Cover design by Elizabeth Maddrey.

Cover art photos ©iStockphoto.com/heather_mcgrath, ©iStockphoto.com/VikaSuh used by permission.

Published in the United States of America by Elizabeth Maddrey. www.ElizabethMaddrey.com

For Tim
The best Valentine a girl could ask for.

1

A nnabelle Elliot typed a quick comment in her code and clicked save before reaching for her ringing phone. Her eyes darted to the clock at the bottom corner of her monitor. Almost lunchtime anyway. She rolled her head on her neck and punched accept on her cell.

"Annabelle Elliot." There was a long pause. Long enough that Annabelle started to pull the phone away from her ear to check the number. Working as a freelance programmer, she didn't have the luxury of ignoring numbers that weren't familiar. There could always be a job at the other end of the line. Which, of course, meant she had to deal with her share of spam calls. "Hello?"

"Hi. Um, is this Anne? Anne Elliot?"

Annabelle's eyebrows lifted. She hadn't gone by Anne in forever. "Yes. Who's calling?"

"Right, sorry. This is Victoria—Tori—Spencer. We knew each other in college? I know it's been a while."

Annabelle fought the laugh building at the back of her throat. That was an understatement. She hadn't thought about

Tori...since graduation? Maybe a little later than that. "Wow. Hi. How are you?"

"Good. I'm good. Engaged, if you can imagine that."

"Congratulations." She checked the time again and stood. She'd hit the fridge while she waited to see if Tori ever got around to the point of the call.

"Thanks. So, I was talking to my step—to Zane Hendricks —and your name came up and...look, I know it's been forever and we weren't exactly besties in college but I could really use a friend, and when he mentioned you...I thought it might be worth a shot."

"Hendricks Security? That Zane Hendricks?" Annabelle was doing some consulting for him, basic stuff, but Hendricks didn't have anyone with solid development skills in-house. Or that's what he'd said. Zane was Tori's step...brother? Had to be brother.

"That's the one. It's a long, weird story, but technically Zane's my step-dad."

Annabelle snickered as she opened the freezer and grabbed a white box at random. Frozen meals all tasted the same, why bother looking at the name and being disappointed? She peeled up a corner of the container, tossed it in the microwave, and hit the pre-programmed button.

Resignation echoed in Tori's laugh. "Yeah, exactly. Anyway, it's short notice, but if you're free on Saturday, my fiancé is having a dinner party—work people who I know only margin-ally—and I'd really love it if you could come. You can bring a guest if you're dating someone. Or married. You know what, never mind."

Something in Tori's tone cut off the automatic thanks-but-no-thanks that had been forming on Annabelle's lips. When you got right down to it, she could use a friend in her life as well. The people she worked for were, at best, solid acquain-tances. Even the ones she did repeat business with. At church, when she went in person instead of just watching online, she was decidedly odd woman out. "Not married, or dating. Can I bring dessert or something?"

Tori's sigh whooshed across the line. "You'll come? Really?"

"Really. Catching up with an old friend and dinner I don't have to microwave myself sounds like just the thing."

"Yay! You don't have to bring anything. Gabe's a bit of a wonder in the kitchen, surprisingly. He won't even let me help. I'll text you the details. Thank you, Anne."

"Annabelle. I gave up on the nickname idea right after graduation. It never took. Half the time I'd forget that was supposed to be me and the other half I needed my legal name anyway. It stopped making sense to fight it."

Tori chuckled. "I had the same thing, but in reverse. Tried, really hard, to switch to Victoria and that hasn't panned out. Though they use it for my by-line at the paper. And if my boss is mad at me. I can't wait to see you again."

"Yeah. Me too." Annabelle hit end and set the phone down on the counter. Not a lie, actually. Talking to Tori had brought back memories of their time on campus. And while, no, they hadn't been best friends, they'd lived on the same floor of the same dorm all four years and had hung out at more than just the floor activities. There'd been potential then. Maybe it was still there.

The microwave chirped the end of the cooking time for her lunch. Annabelle slid the box onto a plate, snagged a fork from the drawer, and carried the steaming meal back to her office, which was actually the second bedroom of her condo. If she was going out this weekend, she'd need to make a little more progress on her current contracts before then. She smiled, even as a little tendril of unease snaked through her. When was the last time she'd had plans that took her out of the house in the evening?

~

ANNABELLE FROWNED at her reflection in the full-length mirror on the back of her closet door. Black slacks, purple blouse, and ballet flats. Did she look like a bruise? It was still chilly. Maybe she should wear a sweater instead? Although her sweaters were all black. Then she'd look like a Goth. Did they still call them that? She buried her face in her hands. She needed to get out more.

Even thinking the words sent her heart into overdrive. Getting out meant crowds. Bumping into people. Close talkers. *Small talk.* Ugh. Maybe she should just call Tori back and let her know she'd changed her mind and wouldn't be coming after all. Annabelle winced as her mother's constant reminders to be polite rang through her mind. Cancelling at the last minute wasn't polite.

She cast a final, longing glance at the pajama pants tossed on the single bed she'd stuffed between the bookshelves lining the walls of her bedroom-slash-library and grabbed a wool blazer in a black and purple houndstooth pattern off a hanger. It turned the outfit into something more appropriate for a business meeting than a dinner party, but it got rid of the bruise comparison. At least in her mind.

Get a grip. And then a move on. There was nothing quite like being late to draw attention to yourself and that was something she absolutely wanted to avoid. If she was lucky, Annabelle could get there, stake out a corner, and chat with Tori the rest of the evening. What had she been thinking when she agreed to this?

She grabbed the zippered pouch that served as her wallet and phone holder, double checked that she had her keys, and forced herself out of the bedroom, through the mostly-barren living room—she really needed to do something about a couch, grownups had couches—and out the door of her condo.

Annabelle twisted the doorknob. Locked. She blew out a breath. That was the hardest step, getting out of the house. Shaking her head, she went down the hall to the elevators. Her car would be happy to see her. If cars had emotions. She was going to say something like that out loud at this party and reveal herself as the biggest dork on the planet. She should just go back...the elevator arrived, its doors opening with a quiet *ding.* Okay. She could do this.

It was a pretty straight shot from Reston to Clifton. Back roads, which made the trek somewhat more enjoyable. Of course, they were all still fairly major roads, for all they weren't the Interstate. Before long, Annabelle turned into the driveway as her phone's GPS announced her arrival. There were only two cars in the paved area in front of the large farmhouse. Either she was still early or everyone else carpooled. She parked next to a shiny, black pickup. It had to be new. Either that or the owner never drove it. Or he washed it religiously. Had to be a he. Not that women couldn't drive trucks, but this truck oozed masculinity.

She patted the roof of her car as she closed the door and hit lock on her key fob. The sedan might be up there in years, but it was still a solid, reliable mode of transportation for the rare occasions when she needed to leave the house.

Swallowing the metallic tang at the back of her throat, Annabelle climbed the steps to the porch and pressed the doorbell before she had a chance to talk herself out of it. It was dinner. With a friend. Sort of friend. She breathed in through her nose and held the air in her lungs, willing her heart to slow and her muscles to quit jumping.

"You're here!" Tori grinned, bouncing on her sock-clad feet. "Come in, come in. I'm so glad you made it. I started worrying you were going to bail at the last minute, and I seriously need someone who doesn't work at Intelligence Associates to talk to. They get going and...it's crazy."

Annabelle stepped in and glanced down at Tori's feet. "Do I need to..."

"What? Oh. Shoes? No, you're fine. Unless you want to. Gabe's pretty laid back. Come on back, we're in the kitchen." Tori shut the door and headed across the sprawling, yet homey, living room.

She focused on her breathing for a few breaths before following. Intelligence Associates? How had she missed that? Or did Tori not mention that her fiancé was Gabe Robertson? Maybe she hadn't said. Annabelle smoothed her blazer. At least she looked professional, so if they made the connection between her and the contracting proposal she'd submitted last night just under the deadline, she wouldn't be embarrassed.

"Gabe, this is Annabelle Elliot, Annabelle, Gabe Robertson, my fiancé." Tori grinned as she said the last word, her left hand flexing on Gabe's arm. "And this is Rick Wentworth. He works with Gabe at IA. They both went to college with us, but neither you nor I really hung in those circles."

The words in Annabelle's throat turned to dust and her gaze flicked to the broad-shouldered man sitting on a stool at the kitchen island, his back to her. Rick? Rick was here? He couldn't be here, he worked in Germany or Afghanistan or something. The edges of her vision began to blur and she took Gabe's outstretched hand on autopilot. His mouth was moving, but the sound was as if she was submerged under twelve feet of water. Rick turned and gave a brief, disinterested nod and the world snapped back into focus. She cleared her throat and offered a tight smile. "Thanks for having me."

Tori shot her a confused look. "You need any help, Gabe?"

He shook his head. "I've got this. Why don't the two of you go relax in the living room? If I need something, I'll holler. Or I'll make Rick earn his keep."

"Whatever." Rick's baritone held the same dry humor he'd

had in college. "I've barely been back in the States two days. Plus I'm on vacation, remember?"

"Vacation isn't something he fully understands, Rick, you ought to know that." Tori grinned. "He takes December off and still manages to work the whole time."

Gabe flicked his fingers at Tori. "Go. No women allowed in the kitchen. New rule."

"That is a rule I can get behind. Come on, Annabelle, we'll turn the fireplace on." Tori hooked her arm through Annabelle's and tugged.

Annabelle flinched but didn't jerk her arm away. What was it with people and touching? As they passed through to the living room, she eased away and angled toward a mission-style armchair done in rich, chocolate leather that offset the honey brown of the oak spindles perfectly. Gabe had good taste. Or was Tori helping him with decorating?

"It's all Gabe. He's lived here a few years. I still have my own apartment near the paper, 'til we're married."

Heat flared across her cheeks and she closed her eyes. Maybe the chair would swallow her whole and put her out of her misery. "I said that out loud."

Tori laughed. "You did. It's okay. I think he's got good taste, too." She paused, tilting her head to one side. "Are you okay?"

No. No, she wasn't okay. Rick was sitting in the next room and didn't even seem to recognize her. It *had* been six years. But still. Somewhere in the back of her mind she'd hoped he was just as unable to get over their breakup as she was. "Sure. Yeah. I'm...kind of out of practice with the getting together with friends thing. How long have you and Gabe been engaged?"

"Four days." Tori grinned. "And we're planning to get married next December, in case you're wondering. So, long engagement. But we really only started dating around Christmas."

"Wow. That's...fast. That's like nine weeks."

Tori shrugged a shoulder. "Like I said, long engagement makes sense. What about you? No one special on the radar?"

Annabelle scoffed. "Who has time? I pretty much work twenty-four-seven. Or six. I try to make it six. But when you're running a one-person software development company, there's always something to do. If I'm not coding, I'm looking for jobs to bid, and if I'm not doing that, I'm actually putting bids together."

"Why not just get a regular job?" Tori winced. "I didn't mean..."

"No, it's a good question...it's just kind of complicated to answer."

2

Rick listened with one ear to Gabe prattling on about the menu for the dinner party while he strained to hear what Tori and Annabelle were talking about. But their voices didn't carry into the kitchen, and Gabe showed no signs of being quiet anytime soon.

"Why are you having this dinner party thing again?"

Gabe stopped chopping the onion he was working on and frowned. "To welcome you home. People in the office miss you, you know."

Rick shook his head. "Who? Other than you, who misses me?"

Gabe picked up his knife again. "Angel might have asked about your arrival date six or seven hundred times."

Angel. That figured. She was a nice woman, but she didn't seem to understand his subtle, and not-so-subtle, signals that he wasn't interested. It wasn't just that she had a daughter, though that was part of it, to be honest. She simply wasn't his type. "Who else?"

Gabe shrugged.

"So, really, this is Angel's attempt to get you to set her up with me in the guise of a welcome home party?" Rick flicked a piece of onion back toward Gabe's chopping board. "I'm surprised you fell for it."

"Tori's been wanting another get together. I didn't think about it very hard, honestly. Welcoming you home was as good a reason as any, right?" Gabe scooped the diced onion into a bowl of other finely chopped vegetables and stirred them together. "Just don't encourage Angel, surely she'll get the idea."

"Right. Like I've been encouraging her up to now? She's relentless." Rick shifted on his stool and eyed Gabe. "So...you're friends with Annabelle?"

"Who? Oh, no, that's Tori's friend. I guess her face is a little familiar from college, but I'd never met her before. Why?"

Rick lifted a shoulder and worked to keep his face impassive. No point letting on that there'd been more between him and Annabelle. Besides, he was over that. And one of these days when he said it, it'd be true. "No reason. Just surprised, I guess, that it's old home week around here."

"You knew her?"

Memories of the walks they used to take around campus long after everyone else was in bed flashed unbidden through his mind. The feel of her hand in his, her lips on his, came rushing back. "A little, yeah. Though she's changed some. Never would've pegged her for a pixie cut."

"Works for her, though. She's got good cheekbones."

Rick nodded. She did. Always had. Though the dark circles under her eyes drew more attention than her bone structure. Gaunt. She looked gaunt. Why? Not that he had any right to know. Not anymore. A knife sliced his heart. Seeing her again...how could everything come rushing back so fast? He was over her. He had to be. "When is everyone getting here?"

Gabe glanced at his watch. "Should be any minute. Why

don't you take the salsa and chips out to the living room? People can munch while we wait for everything to be ready."

RICK LEANED back in his chair. Gabe could cook, that was certain. Conversation around the table had been interesting, ranging all over the map from some of the programming challenges IA was facing to whether or not the Caps had a shot at the Stanley Cup this year. He'd watched Annabelle when she wasn't looking—which was most of the time. She was barely a shadow of the vivacious girl he'd loved in college. Though she still had the quickest mind he'd ever encountered. She'd solved two of their code issues—problems that had been plaguing the in-house teams for months—in under twenty minutes while sitting at the dining room table. And the solution was elegant.

"Let's play Taboo." Tori dropped her napkin beside her plate and scooted her chair back.

Good-natured groans echoed around the table, but gradually, everyone made their way into the living room and formed into teams. Annabelle hovered in the doorway, arms crossed, and whispered to Tori, who shook her head and patted Annabelle's arm.

"Okay, Annabelle's going to be the buzzer, to keep us honest." Tori grinned and set the game's box on the coffee table.

Rick arched a brow and leaned closer to Tori. "She doesn't want to play?"

Tori shrugged. "She said she'd rather not, and was going to leave. This was the only way I could get her to hang a little while longer."

Angel scooted closer to Rick on the couch so their legs touched. "I haven't played this in ages. What about you?"

Rick started to frown then caught Gabe's eye and bit back a sigh. He could try to play nice. He'd much rather engage Annabelle in conversation...though it seemed unlikely that she'd care. *Move on.* He was moving on. Maybe Angel was a step in that direction? "I can't think of the last time I played, though we did have a rather rowdy game along these lines the first year we were overseas. Remember that, Gabe?"

Gabe laughed. "That is...not a memory for mixed company."

"The words were considerably more off-color than the boxed deck, but what do you expect when you're hunkered down in a war zone?" Rick grinned. "But I guess those days are over once you're married, right Gabe? Then it'll be completely up to Jake and me to handle the on-site operations."

"That doesn't seem fair. I'm perfectly happy to spend time overseas—you're based out of Germany most of the time, right?" Tori shuffled the word cards, bending them into a smooth bridge to slide the deck back together.

Gabe patted Tori's leg. "Sure we are. And if you want to come, we'll figure it out. It isn't as if there aren't plenty of spouses and families stationed overseas right along with the soldiers."

"Yeah, well, I'm not convinced that's a good idea. Too much distraction from the work at hand." Rick shook his head and reached for a card.

Gabe snickered. "Says the man without a wife or girlfriend."

"That's true." Rick's gaze flicked up and landed on Annabelle. "I have no wife."

~

RICK STARED at the logs in the fireplace. The evening had ended up more fun than he'd anticipated. Though to be fair, he'd had low expectations. Angel wasn't even as annoying as usual.

Maybe her daughter staying with her ex was a positive change. Or maybe time was mellowing her. Either way, their conversation had been almost pleasant. Seeing Annabelle again had been...there were too many possibilities to settle on a single word. He rubbed his chest, as if that would make the ache go away.

"You okay?" Gabe paused in the doorway to the living room, a steaming mug in his hand. "Want some tea? The kettle's still hot."

"Sure. Tea sounds good, but I can get it, if you're heading up."

Gabe shook his head. "I can hang for a bit. Maybe it'll help with jet lag next week."

Rick chuckled. "Nothing's going to help with jet lag. You just set your mind to dealing with the new schedule and do it."

"Muscle through, huh?"

"Basically." Rick stood. "Grab a seat, I'll go get my tea and you can remind me why I'm filling in at the office for you instead of taking a real vacation."

Gabe's laughter followed him into the kitchen. At least he didn't have to go in every day, but he'd come stateside to rest and relax, not take over the bureaucratic nonsense that Gabe usually handled. The tea bags were still out on the counter. He dropped one in a mug and poured steaming water over it without checking the kind. It was tea. It all pretty much tasted the same.

"You don't have to go in if it's a problem." Gabe was slouched down in a chair, his sock-clad feet up on the coffee table.

"It's not a problem. I don't know what I'd do with all that free time anyway. I just like to give you a hard time." Rick resumed his place on the couch and stretched out. "Besides, if at least one of us isn't there, the brass at the Pentagon is going to spend the whole time calling you, keeping you from helping

Jake when he needs it. Though the team over there's really quite good. I don't know that he'll need much help."

"We've come a long way, haven't we?"

Rick sipped the hot liquid, his eyebrows lifting at the orangey flavor. "You said it. What is this?"

"Some Christmas blend Tori gave me. Orange, clove, and cinnamon or something like that. It's hot and doesn't have caffeine." Gabe eyed Rick over the top of his mug. "You going to tell me about Annabelle?"

A hot ball of lead settled in Rick's stomach. "Nothing to tell."

"Dude."

Rick broke eye contact and stared into his drink. It was all in the past. Where it belonged. Seeing her again had been a shock—no, a surprise—but it wasn't as if he was still in love with her. That would be ridiculous, and he wasn't going to be ridiculous. Maybe only a little. Gabe's gaze continued to bore into him. He set the tea aside and stared into the flames. "We were engaged for about two days our senior year. I was convinced she was the woman God had for me."

Gabe's mug hit the arm of his chair with a *thud*. "What? How did I not know that?"

"You and I were never that tight. Not in college. I was the token geek in the frat, everyone knew that." One side of his mouth poked up. "Someone had to help keep the GPA above passing. I never even had to go out of my way to hide our relationship from the guys in the frat who would've made fun."

"So what happened?"

"She broke it off."

"Why?"

Rick reached for his tea. Having something in his hands had to be better than clenching them into fists like he usually did when he thought about it. "We'd just started hammering out details for IA. I guess the thought of being married to someone trying to get a business off the ground—especially this type of business—was too risky for her. I'd planned to ask you and Jake about hiring her to head up development, as you saw tonight, she's got amazing skills on the computer, but Hewitt came on board and before I had a chance to think twice, she was giving me back the ring."

Gabe tapped the side of his mug. "That explains some things about that first year."

Rick winced. "Yeah...sorry about that. I...should've told you guys. Or at least you and Jake, Hewitt wouldn't have cared. But it was easier to throw myself into work, snarl at anyone who questioned, and jump at the opportunity to get overseas when it presented itself."

"Turns out you have a knack for interfacing with the military."

"Yeah. I guess it worked out for the best in the end." Hadn't it? He liked his life. He ran through his usual mental litany of reminders, the ones he pulled out every time he started dwelling on Annabelle and the life he could have—should have—had. The one with her in it. Living overseas was interesting. His work was challenging and meaningful. And if he'd been married six years ago he would likely have made very different decisions. You didn't throw yourself into a war zone as a newlywed. Usually.

"I'll tell Tori..."

"Don't. Don't tell Tori anything, okay? It's fine. If she turns up here, or around the office or whatever, it'll be fine. She's out of my system."

"Is she?"

"It's been six years. Of course she is." She had to be. Rick frowned into the tea before setting it aside. "Maybe I'll see if Angel wants to grab dinner one night this week."

Gabe said nothing as he stood. He crossed to the stairs and stopped, one foot on the first step. "Make sure you're doing things for the right reason. And don't forget to turn off the fire before you head to bed."

Rick nodded. Was he really going to ask Angel on a date? She wasn't his type. Of course, the one woman in the world who was exactly his type had broken his heart. So maybe the man with nothing whole to offer shouldn't be so picky.

3

I have no wife. Why had he been looking at her when he said it? Annabelle stared at the ceiling over her bed. Six years. She'd figured he'd be married by now, happily raising kids with his adoring wife. Was he really still unmarried? Why was that? His job? What did it matter? That ship had long since moved out into open water, been smashed by a hurricane, and washed up in pieces on a deserted island. She shouldn't still be losing sleep over him.

She rolled to her side and frowned at the clock. Close enough to morning, she might as well get up. Throwing her legs over the side of the bed, she stood and reached up, stretching onto her toes. She eased back down, lowering her palms flat to the floor and relaxing as her hamstrings protested. Annabelle worked through a few more slow stretches to get the blood flowing then shuffled to the kitchen. She dug an English muffin out of the bag on top of her microwave and dropped it into the toaster before pressing a coffee pod into the machine, positioning an extra large mug under the spout, and hitting brew. While she waited, she went into the her office and booted up her computer. The three monitors blinked to life. Stretched across them was a photo of her and Rick, arms around each other, laughing. One of the photographers for the college paper had snapped the shot, intending to use it as part of a feature on campus life. It had never run, but he'd delivered on his promise to get her a copy of the picture.

Six years.

Maybe it was time to change her computer's wallpaper.

If only it was as easy to change her heart.

She opened her email and cringed. She was going to need coffee to wade through the mess. Yet another reason not to leave the house—you got behind on your communication. She'd left her phone in her pocket for most of the night. People seemed to think it was rude if she checked every time it chimed. No one ever seemed to want to make exceptions for independent contractors, either.

Back in the kitchen, she spread butter on the toasted muffin, dumped two packets of artificial sweetener and a generous slosh of creamer into her coffee, and carried it all back to the office. She tucked a leg under her as she sat and bit into the crunchy toast, mentally sorting the email into groups for deleting, reading, and responding to...Tori?

With a smile, she opened that email. Even if leaving the house was a questionable idea, reconnecting with Tori had been pleasant. Cultivating that friendship was worthwhile.

Annabelle!

It was such fun to hang with you last night. Thank you for coming! But! I have to know what's up between you and Rick. He had some...let's go with not-quite-friendly things to say about you after you left. Nothing salacious, mind you, but there has to be a history there. How did I not know this?! And seriously, the way he looked at you all night? I need the scoop. Lunch? Say you'll do lunch with me—any day this week. I'll meet you somewhere. Text me. Promise.

-T

She snickered. Tori'd been addicted to exclamation marks in college. Why hadn't a job as a real journalist fixed that? Lunch. She blew out a breath and checked the time. She could easily make it to church and suggest lunch after...but did Tori even go to church still? Leaving the house two days in a row...her stomach twisted. It'd probably be better to put off lunch until a weekday. Or indefinitely. No. No, she was getting back on the friendship train. Tori was reaching out, Annabelle owed it to her, and to herself, to meet her half-way.

Opening a web browser, Annabelle navigated to her church's website and hit play. She'd stream the recording of their Saturday night service, sort through email, and get a head start on tomorrow's workload. That would free up time for lunch with Tori.

Which just left figuring out how much to tell. Six years. And Rick still hadn't been friendly? She couldn't blame him. Not really. But...maybe she'd just tell Tori the whole thing. It might be nice to have someone else know the details. Her gaze drifted to the photo on her monitor and a lump formed in her throat. Why did everything in life have to be so complicated?

MONDAY MORNING'S alarm blared in her ear. Annabelle fumbled for her phone, finally managing to swipe her finger across the screen to quiet the noise. She pried open one eye and stared at the glowing numbers on the clock until they resolved into something that made sense. Seven o'clock. Too early. Did she have any morning appointments?

With a sigh, she propped herself on one elbow and detached her phone from the charger so she could pull up her calendar. Lunch with Tori at one—who ate that late? Journalists, apparently. But nothing until then. Which meant she could sleep another hour. Maybe two. She set another alarm and snuggled back under the covers. Why was the second day after a night with no sleep so much harder than the day after? Was it because you'd had enough sleep to realize how truly sleep deprived you were?

She flung an arm over her eyes. Two more hours. Except...according to the notification window on her phone's lock screen when she'd checked her calendar, there'd been fifty-two new emails. How could she get that many emails overnight? Most of them were probably spam or ads, notifications from blogs she kept up with, that sort of thing. But still. Fifty-two. A chime sounded from her phone. Make that fifty-three. She flopped over onto her side. It'd take at least an hour to wade through them. And she hadn't made as much extra progress yesterday as she'd planned. The day had been warm for the last weekend of January, so she'd snuck out on the balcony and read. It wasn't sneaking, really. She didn't work on Sundays as a rule. She worshipped God and rested. A day of rest. Which meant...the phone chimed again...which meant dragging herself out of bed and getting a start on the day.

Annabelle took a quick shower while coffee brewed and an English muffin toasted. She threw on black slacks and a lightweight sweater in a color that reminded her of raspberries. It was brighter than it looked on the computer when she ordered it, but it fit and was comfortable so...it was good enough. She ran her fingers through her short crop of hair, rubbed moisturizer on her cheeks, and gave a quick nod to herself in the mirror, laughter sparkling in her brown eyes.

By the time she was halfway through the new email, she was down to the bottom of her third cup of coffee and it was creeping up on nine a.m. Her cell buzzed on the desk.

"Annabelle Elliot."

"Hi, Ms. Elliot. This is Gabe Robertson from IA, Inc. Do you have a minute?"

Her eyebrows lifted. He was awfully formal for someone

she'd had to buzz multiple times during the game they'd played at his dinner party. Apparently he was incapable of reading a word silently and not saying it when the pressure was on. "Of course. What can I do for you?"

He chuckled. "It was nice to meet you on Saturday. I'm told we probably met once or twice in college, but..."

"Please. That was a million years ago and we weren't exactly in the same circles. I lived in the computer science building most of those four years. Thanks again for having me."

"My pleasure." He paused and cleared his throat. "I'm actually calling about the proposal you submitted."

Her heart rate accelerated. Was he going to turn her down because of her connection to Rick? Did he even know about her connection with Rick? "Yes?"

"We've looked it over and it's compelling. We'd like to offer the contract with one minor change. The nature of our work, as you can imagine, is highly sensitive. Even what isn't directly classified can't leave the building. So we'd need you to work onsite, in the Arlington office, for the duration."

Annabelle bit her lips to hold in a groan. That was the one thing she'd been worried about when she submitted the proposal. Could she go into an office every day? Work with all those people around her?

"Annabelle?"

"Sorry. I...yeah, that's okay. I knew it was a possibility. When do you need me to start?" She opened her calendar and considered the coming week. She had a little more work to do to tie up loose ends on her current work. There were a handful of bids out, but nothing that would take much time, even if she got the work. She could handle them in the evenings, on weekends. The IA contract was a foot in the door to bigger, more lucrative contracts that would allow her to relax just a little and spend less time hustling to ensure her income pipeline didn't dry up completely.

"Is it possible for you to start tomorrow? The sooner we can start showing progress, the better it's going to be for us. If that's too fast..."

"No, it's fine. Tomorrow will work."

"Great. I'll have Angel—you met her on Saturday, too—shoot you an email with the pertinent details for tomorrow, as well as the contract. Just bring your signed copy with you in the morning."

"Will do. Thanks." Annabelle ended the call and did a wiggling dance in her chair. She'd gotten the contract. Working in the office was...a major negative. But she'd get through it. She would. She had to.

"I'M SO glad you could make it. I know it's a little late for lunch, but it's the way my schedule worked today." Tori wrapped Annabelle in a tight hug. Annabelle stiffened. It was a default reaction, though she tried to stop herself. "Not a hugger?"

Annabelle eased back. "Sorry."

Tori waved the apology away. "Don't worry about it. Here, I almost ordered you a sweet tea, but I wasn't sure if that was something you still enjoyed."

Annabelle took the menu. "Not as much as I used to, but it sounds perfect. What's good here?"

"Everything."

She frowned. "Seriously?"

Tori shrugged. "I've never had something I didn't like. Is that a better way to put it? But since it's an Irish pub, you have to go for something Irish. I'm sure the sandwiches and stuff are good, but get the potato leek soup or the shepherd's pie."

"Fish and chips?"

Tori wrinkled her nose. "Not a fish fan, haven't tried them.

But sure, go nuts. Now, spill it. What's the deal with you and Rick?"

Annabelle chuckled, though a solid knot settled in her stomach. They hadn't even ordered drinks yet. She glanced around the dim restaurant. Not that she expected to see anyone she knew, but the IA offices were within walking distance so it wasn't unreasonable to be cautious.

"They've all eaten. IA's an early lunch crowd. If that's what you're worried about." One corner of Tori's mouth quirked up. "Or do you not want to talk about it? I won't push."

The waitress appeared at the table and took their orders, disappearing again before Annabelle had completely made up her mind. "I...we dated for most of college. We met in a programming class my second semester and hit it off."

"All right, I remember talk—generically—of your boyfriend. That was Rick?"

Annabelle nodded.

"So what happened?"

She smiled as the waitress returned with their drinks. What had happened? So many little things. "He proposed spring semester of our senior year."

"What? You were *engaged*?"

Annabelle winced and held a finger to her lips. "Shh. Yeah, we were. For about three days. And then..." Here's where it got tricky. Did she explain the whole mess or just skim the surface? There was no reason, really, to drag Dr. Blackburn into it. Except...looking back...she sighed. "Did you ever meet Dr. Blackburn?"

Tori pursed her lips and slowly shook her head. "That doesn't ring a bell."

"Figures. She was a computer science professor. Very, let's go with 'passionate,' about women in computers and helping them to achieve success in a field that's continually dominated by men."

"Mmhmm."

"Anyway, I looked up to her. A lot. She took me—and the handful of other women in the major—on as mentees. When she found out about the engagement she was horrified. She reminded me of the career goals I had and convinced me that Rick wasn't going to support me in them. She painted this picture of, I don't know, an eighteenth century marriage where I was the little woman, barefoot and pregnant in the kitchen for the rest of my life. I didn't know what Rick planned for after graduation. We'd talked about it, a little, but it was all the usual things. He must've been talking in depth with Gabe about IA, Inc., but we'd never really discussed what it would look like when we were married. I mean, a startup? Even if I wasn't barefoot in the kitchen, the possibility of being the one supporting both of us was real. So, between the fact that my parents had made it clear they weren't excited about the prospect of me getting married right away and Dr. Blackburn's dire predictions, I broke off our engagement. Said I needed some time. He avoided me for the rest of the term and disappeared after graduation."

"Wow. I just...wow." Tori shook out her napkin and set it in her lap as the server came with their meals. "Can we pray?"

Annabelle nodded and bowed her head. Since when did Tori pray out loud, in public? The blessing was brief, but clearly heartfelt. The aroma of batter fried fish and malt vinegar rose from the plate in front of her. She mumbled "amen" and reached for the salt shaker.

"And you haven't seen him since?" Tori scooped a forkful of creamy mashed potatoes off the top of her shepherd's pie.

"Not until Saturday."

"Hmmm. And you're not dating anyone?"

Annabelle shook her head and cut open a fish filet, letting the steam escape, sending more of the mouth watering aroma wafting into her face.

"So...have you dated anyone since?"

"What are you, the dating fairy?"

Tori chuckled. "I'll take that as a no."

"It's not a no...not really. I've dated. Some."

"Mmmhmm. When was your last date?"

A year, at least. More? There hadn't been anyone serious since Rick. Not even at her first—and last—office job. Despite what her then-manager had seemed to think about the potential for a relationship. "I'm busy. I work for myself, that doesn't leave a lot of time for anything else. Not if I want to keep a roof over my head."

"But now you have a contract with IA, right? So that'll help. And with Gabe in Germany for the next three weeks, you'll have plenty of time to rekindle things with Rick."

"What?"

"What what?"

"Gabe's out of town? But he called me this morning to explain about the contract. Working in the office. All of that." Her hands were suddenly clammy. She couldn't work directly for Rick. It simply wasn't possible.

Tori smiled, a touch of sympathy in her eyes. "They have phones in Germany. Actually, Gabe's cell works internationally. Makes more sense when you're traveling the globe. I thought you knew."

Annabelle shook her head, her food congealing in her stomach. She pushed her plate away, the once-pleasing fragrance now causing her abdominal muscles to clench. She hadn't signed anything yet, or turned it in. She could call Gabe and say something had come up. Except...this was still her chance to move into the world of more profitable contracting and maybe, for once, do more than scrape by. Wouldn't it be nice not to have to dip into her trust fund anymore and have the freedom ignore the baggage that came with every one of her father's disbursements? She needed to see this through.

Rick was an owner. Surely he was going to be too busy to micromanage a programming project.

She took a long sip of sweet tea and poked the fish with her fork. Time to change the subject. "Do you have a date in mind yet for the wedding?"

~

"HI, DAD." Annabelle clipped her bluetooth headset around her ear before merging into the Arlington traffic. Once Tori got started talking about wedding ideas, it had been easy enough to smile, nod in all the right places, and tune her out, spinning through various scenarios that didn't have her working with Rick for the next month. None of them were particularly palatable.

Her father cleared his throat. "Your mother and I are planning to spend some time in the Georgetown house this month. Why don't you join us? I know it's not far from where you are, but it's right there in the heart of the action, not out there in the suburbs. Honestly, I don't know why you chose that place." Disdain dripped from his tongue. As usual.

She didn't bother to sigh. "It's what I could afford, Dad. We've been through this. I'm not interested in relying on your money or your connections."

"Right. Fine. So, we'll see you on Saturday? I'll have Carmela prepare your room. Your mother—oh, fine, here's your mother."

"Annabelle, darling, there are so many lovely parties planned this month, mostly Valentine's themed, but if your young man can't make it, I'm sure we can drum up some dates for you without any problem. Be sure you bring—you know what, *don't* bring any cocktail gowns. That'll give us an excuse to go shopping. My treat. And maybe—"

"Mom, stop. I can't take a month off right now. Or even a week."

"What do you mean? Of course you can. You're your own boss."

She clenched the steering wheel. Why did she keep expecting them to understand? "Yes, that's true. But I just signed a new contract and the proposal had some strict timing requirements. Since I'm not only the boss but the only employee, that means I'm going to be very busy starting tomorrow."

Her mother's breath huffed out. Annabelle could picture the bewildered expression that likely dominated her mother's features. "Honestly, Annabelle, that's very inconvenient."

"I know. I'm sorry." Pain began to throb behind her left eye.

"Well. We'll at least need you to come for dinner. You can bring your young man."

"Mom. There's no young man to bring. And I'll have to see what my work schedule is like when the contract's started. I'm guessing I'll be putting in some long hours. I'll let you know, all right?"

"Of course. Do you need money? I can talk to your fath—"

"I'm fine, but thanks. Give Dad my love. Love you, Mom." She pressed end before her mom had a chance to try and extend the call any further.

Being in the office with Rick every day was going to be a picnic compared to a month with her parents in Georgetown.

4

"You did what?" Rick glared at the phone on Gabe's desk at the Intelligence Associates, Inc. office. "I'm sure I didn't hear you say you awarded a contract without discussing it with me and Jake first."

"Jake doesn't care about the software end of things, never has. You know that."

Rick crossed his arms. It was lucky Gabe was in Germany. Rick hadn't felt the urge to punch someone in quite some time, but it was coming back. Rapidly. "Okay, that handles Jake. What about me? The person who joined the team specifically to head up product development, back when that was our goal."

The connection crackled.

"You there?"

"Yeah, I'm here. Look, man, it's not like we got a ton of submissions in the first place. But of the handful we got? Hers is, hands down, the best. The fact that Tori knows her, and you do too, not to mention how she solved those problems on Saturday so easily, is just icing on the cake. Regardless of how poorly things turned out between the two of you, the fact that you got as close as you did speaks volumes for her character. If we hire someone off the street, we don't know what we're getting. It's a risk I'd rather avoid if I can, and this seems like a providentially-supplied way to do just that."

God brought Annabelle back into his life? He'd placed the blame for that fully on the other side of the spiritual realm. He loved her. The dinner party had made that abundantly clear. But at least when he wasn't around her he could live some semblance of a normal life. He could try to pretend he'd moved on. With her in the office...Rick tapped his fingers together. "Can I at least look at the other bids?"

"They're in the shared drive. But I talked to Annabelle this morning, she's starting tomorrow. I'd need a compelling reason to change that. Something that goes beyond a little discomfort."

"All right. I...does she know I'm spearheading the project?"

"She knows she's working in the office and that you're there."

Rick closed his eyes, his stomach sinking into his shoes. "Gabe."

"What? You're a professional. So is she. Make it work. We need this program operational by the end of February."

Right. Focus on the mission. "Got it. As long as this isn't some misguided attempt at matchmaking."

Gabe's chuckle was dry and tinged with fatigue. "You know me better than that, don't you?"

"Probably."

"Good. She'll be there at nine tomorrow morning. Play nice, okay, Rick?"

"Like you said, I'm a professional. Try to keep Jake in line while you're over there, will you? He needs help with that sometimes." When Gabe signed off, Rick punched the speaker button to end the call and scrubbed his hands over his face. Be a professional. Maybe if he just went out of his way to avoid her he could manage that. He looked up at a knock on the door. "Come in."

Angel pushed open the door and took one step into the room. She stood there fidgeting. What was it with the woman? If she wasn't throwing herself at him, she was acting like she was worried he was going to hit her. He gave a slight smile and waited.

"I have a pile of message slips. A lot of them are for Gabe, but he didn't say...should I email them to him? It's kind of a long way for him to be returning calls. Most of them don't seem urgent..."

Rick stuck out his hand. "I'll handle them. Anything I can't take care of, I'll pass on to Gabe."

"Okay. Great. Good." She gave him the slips and turned toward the door.

"Angel?"

She spun around. "Yeah?"

Just do it. Before he changed his mind, he needed to just do it. If nothing else, it might get his mind off Annabelle. "Are you free for dinner on Saturday?"

Pink crawled up her neck and bloomed on her cheeks as she winced. "Oh. Well. Um. I..."

Great. Perfect. He'd totally misread the signals. "Never mind. I'm sorry."

"No. I...it's just my daughter. With the new custody thing, weekends...I'm trying to keep them open in case she wants to come home for an extra day. I don't want to be the one saying no. I could do a weeknight?"

"Sure. Okay. Tomorrow?" That would get it over with. Or leave things open for setting something else up if, by some miracle, it went well. He was only in the States for a month. That was long enough to decide if anything could happen between them. Though he'd already pretty much ruled it out. So why was he doing this?

"Yeah, great. Um. What time?"

"Why don't we just leave from here? We can grab a bite at

the pub, and that way we're not far from our cars. Makes it easier."

Her face fell an instant before she smiled. "That...makes sense. So, thanks. I guess I should get back to the phones."

He lifted a hand and turned his attention to the thick wad of pink call slips in his hand. What did he just do?

RICK STRETCHED out on the couch at Gabe's house and stared into the fire crackling on the hearth. Being back in the office was completely different from the work he was used to. He wasn't, technically, filling in for Gabe. He was simply supposed to do his job in the office here, and pick up any urgent matters that Gabe would normally handle. And even with all that, he wasn't going to be in every day. Or he didn't have to be. This was vacation time more than anything. It just happened that he didn't have much planned in the way of time off, so he might as well get the new software update off the ground. Originally, his sister and brother-in-law were going to be in town. They'd had a change of plans, ending up in England. And though they'd asked him to come visit them there, he'd understood it wasn't the right time. Not with them just settling in, finding a place to live, getting new jobs underway. They'd be tripping over him.

And so here he was, staring down the prospect of managing a project Annabelle would be delivering. How was he going to survive seeing her every day without letting on how he still felt? He had to keep it hidden—she'd made her feelings clear, he wasn't going to let her see him as the pathetic soul who clung to love that walked away years in the past. Even if it was the truth.

She probably didn't need him to manage anything. She'd always been the best at what she did. Even in college, she'd outperformed everyone in the department. Even most of the professors. She was fast and creative and had the innate ability to understand a problem and see a solution within minutes. He'd leave her to her own devices—be cordial if he couldn't avoid her—and she'd be finished with the project and gone before his heart had a chance to betray him.

Why was she freelancing?

That had never been her goal and was the reason he'd never really mentioned the idea of IA to her when they were together. Why he'd wanted to make sure he could offer her at least a Vice President-level position, not just ask her to come be a programmer, before he laid it all out. She'd been adamant from day one that she wanted to work for a major national or, better yet, international software development company. Someplace that people would recognize the minute you said the company name. Not for status. Status had never been her goal either. But security.

Despite coming from wealth, Annabelle had prized the notion of earning her own way in the world and doing so in a manner that never left her questioning whether she could pay her own way, with no help from her father. When had she decided to do the exact opposite?

And why?

The questions plagued him, but it was unlikely he'd ever have the answers. He'd been so sure of them, their future together. He'd known in his heart that marrying Annabelle was what God intended and that together they'd do great things for Him. That had been the last time he'd been sure of God's will. To have been that wrong? He was clearly incapable of hearing and understanding what God wanted from him. And that was a hard thing to realize.

Gabe thought God brought Annabelle to IA? No. They might be working together in the office for a time, but Rick was going to keep as much distance as he could. He'd painstakingly glued the pieces of his heart back together six years ago and the aching, scarred vessel wasn't able to withstand another beating.

5

Annabelle took a deep breath and refused to fidget with the waistband of the khaki slacks she'd finally donned after discarding four other outfits. Why hadn't she asked what the dress code was? Dumb question. She'd been too shell-shocked to realize Rick was working in the office rather than Gabe. Hadn't Tori said Rick was here on vacation? Apparently his ideas about relaxing had changed in the last six years. Not that she was one to talk. She hadn't purposefully taken more than Sunday off in...entirely too long to count.

But time off meant visiting family—they'd never forgive her if she didn't—and that was not something she cared to do. Not until she could go home a proven success, show her dad that she didn't need his money or the strings he and her mom tied to it. She'd finally shaken off the guilt that came with knowing and following her own mind, and though she'd been too late to save her relationship with Rick, she still had a chance to show her parents that she knew what she was doing. This project was a major stepping stone toward that goal, so it was time to stop dithering by the elevators and just go.

She pulled open the heavy glass door and stopped in her

tracks. Rick was there, with one hip perched on the receptionist's desk, his hands moving wildly as he explained something
that was, apparently, hilarious. At least if the woman—was it
Angel?—was to be believed. Her ringing laugh filled the space.
Now what? Wait 'til they're done? Was it interrupting if they
were having their...flirtation, there was no other word...in the
main lobby?

Annabelle cleared her throat.

Rick glanced over his shoulder and stiffened when their
eyes met. What was that in his gaze? Pain? Couldn't be. Not
after so long. He scooted off the desk, gave a brisk nod to the
receptionist, and strode down the hall with his hands stuffed in
his pockets.

"Oh, hi. Annabelle, right?" Angel smiled, though her gaze
darted down the hall, following Rick's departure.

"That's me. I'll be working in the office through the end of
February, unless I get things finished sooner than that."
Annabelle hitched the strap of her laptop case higher on her
shoulder. "Someone should be expecting me."

"Yep. Hang on one second." Angel punched buttons on the
phone in front of her, waited, then spoke into her headset.
"Miss Elliot is here...okay...sure thing."

Annabelle fought the urge to tap her foot. It was bad
enough that she had to work in an office, but Rick had seen her
come in. Why couldn't he just stay, like a grown up, and skip
this whole pretense?

"Benick James, our Office Manager-slash-HR director, will
be right out. You can have a seat, if you like."

HR. Right. Paperwork. What a waste. Even as a contractor
she was going to end up spending half of her first day mucking
around with paperwork? Why hadn't they sent her whatever it
was she needed to fill out? With what she hoped would pass as
a friendly smile, Annabelle crossed the room to the row of
serviceable black chairs, dropped her laptop bag on the closest

one, then turned to study the framed maps that graced the wall. Markings showed...she leaned in, squinting...were those battle lines? She shook her head, smiling slightly as she finally identified some of the major campaigns of the Napoleonic wars. Rick had been fascinated by Napoleon in college. Either that hadn't changed or their decorator had stumbled into irony.

"Miss Elliot?"

Annabelle turned. The man had a quiet step. She hadn't heard him approach. "Yes. Hi."

"Benick James, everyone just calls me Ben. Pleasure to have you aboard." He extended his hand for a perfunctory shake. "Come this way and we'll get all the paperwork handled, then I'll pass you off to your team."

Team? Her eyebrows lifted. "I hadn't realized there was already a team. The RFP..."

"Yeah, that's part of what we'll go over." He smiled, lighting up his whole face and removing the previous dour expression completely. Without it, he was a good looking man. Maybe in his thirties? Definitely prior military if his hairstyle and build were any indication. That was reasonable, given the contracts IA sought. They probably had a number of employees who had transitioned out of the military.

She sighed and grabbed her laptop. This was part of what had kept her from looking at contracts with the larger corporations. After her experiences the first year out of college she'd realized that those companies had zero—less than zero—loyalty when it came to their employees. Making a name for herself wasn't going to be possible at a place like that if she also wanted to hold on to her ethics. Since then, she'd stayed far away from contracts that were subject to change without notice. She'd thought a smaller, more agile company like IA would be immune to that. How wrong she'd been had yet to be determined, but she wasn't handing over her signed contract until it was clear.

"Here we are." Ben pushed open the door to a small, cluttered office and gestured for her to enter. "Grab a seat at the table, I'll get the papers."

Table? Annabelle frowned. Was that...? Yes. Buried under piles of books and folders was, in fact, a table crammed into the corner of the office. She grabbed the single empty chair in the room and dragged it closer.

"Just shove that stack out of the way. Sorry. I always mean to spend time cleaning up in here, and then get distracted." Ben scooped up papers and books and plopped them on top of other piles, leaving them to wobble precariously. "Here we are. This is all basic information for tax purposes, why don't you start with that?"

She shook her head. "I'd like to know what changed with the contract before we go any further."

His eyebrows shot up. "Okay. Maybe I should get Mr. Wentworth and have him explain?"

"I don't think that's necessary. At least, not yet. Why don't you start and if we need him, we'll readdress. You mentioned a team? I bid this as a sole provider. Which is, I might add, how it was advertised."

Ben patted the pocket of his dress shirt before plucking out a pair of rimless glasses. He hooked the wires over his ears and flipped open the folder in front of him. The glasses added a dimension to him that was...attractive...but there was no point in letting her thoughts wander in that direction. She worked here, or at least was planning to, if they weren't trying to hose her. Office romances were never a good idea. Not that she was looking for romance in the first place.

"Aha. Here we are." Ben spun the folder so she could read and tapped a paragraph in the middle. "It's not so much that you're part of a development team as you have the resources of a team available to you. My guess is Mr. Wentworth expected you'd want their help since the timeframe is so short."

She scanned the words. It was familiar—clearly that language had been part of the RFP—but she'd dismissed it before putting her proposal together. "It's not required?"

"What isn't?"

Annabelle tapped the paper. "Using the team. It's not required?"

"No. But..."

"Okay, great. I'll decline." She flashed a tight smile and clicked her pen, bending to the first sheet of personal data.

"Decline...they've already been told they're being re-tasked. Mr. Wentworth had a meeting first thing."

"Yes, well, perhaps he should have read my proposal more carefully. I bid a single programmer for the entire job. I have a project plan in place. Throwing more people into the mix is, at this point, simply going to cost more time and complicate matters. Surely he can un-re-task them?" She continued filling in the data, flipping to the next page when she reached the bottom.

Ben cleared his throat. "I'll just go have a word with him while you work on those papers."

"KNOCK KNOCK?" Ben James leaned against the doorframe of the temporary office assigned to Annabelle.

She hit save and glanced up. "Yeah?"

"A group of us are going for lunch. I thought you might like to come along?"

Annabelle sighed and made another mental tick in the negative column of working in an office. Bad enough she had to deal with people, but now they wanted her to be social? "I really wasn't planning..."

"Oh, come on. We won't be long—we're just hitting the taco joint across the parking lot. You'll be back inside thirty minutes. And it'll give you a chance to meet the rest of the IA nerds."

"But I'm..."

"Grab your wallet. You can't sit here by yourself the entire first day. It's not right."

It was clear there was no point in arguing, no matter how much she wanted to. Was this the same as hanging out with Tori? A step in the direction of making friends, getting involved in life again? Six years. She'd spent the last six years hiding from life, holed up in her office for the first and in her condo for the last five. Not hiding. Focused. She'd been—was—focused on her goals, right? But that didn't mean she had to be a hermit. She let her gaze roam over his friendly face, the impish gleam in his eye that hinted of the same off-the-wall humor she typically enjoyed. "All right. Thirty minutes."

He drew an X over his heart and grinned. "Great. You're going to like the crew."

That seemed...unlikely. But she could probably at least tolerate them for lunch. "These aren't the same people I was supposed to be working with, are they?"

"Most of 'em, yes."

Her stomach sank. "Maybe I should..."

"Nope, you agreed." He studied her, frowning. "They have plenty of work to do, if that's what you're worried about. To be honest? Most of them were ticked that Wentworth was moving them to your project."

Her chuckle held no mirth. "Then I guess it's good I declined."

"You all right?"

She slipped her wallet out of her laptop bag and stood, pausing to grab her phone and tuck it into her pocket. "Yeah, I'm fine. I just...I'm not good at social situations in the best of circumstances. This sounds like I'm already setup for failure. You know?"

Ben clapped her on the shoulder. "You'll be fine. It's just tacos. And since they were all getting on the elevator when I headed over here to convince you to come, you're probably going to be stuck with just me for most of the time anyway."

"Sorry."

"Don't be. I'm not." He gave her another grin. "So, tell me everything I need to know about Annabelle Elliot in one hundred words or less."

She laughed. "That's an awfully strict word count."

"Oooh, down to ninety-four."

They chatted amiably on the way to the taco place, arriving after everyone else had started eating. She didn't mind. Many of them were preoccupied with other conversations, giving her the opportunity to slip in at the end of the table and observe.

Ben took the chair next to her, bowing his head over his meal before slicing into his burrito.

"Hey, Ben." The man on the other side of Annabelle leaned across the table. "Did you hear Rick and Angel are going out?"

Ben frowned. "Alan."

Alan held up his hands. "I'm just saying."

"Have you met our new contractor, Annabelle? Annabelle, this is Alan, our company gossip." Ben sawed a bite off his burrito and popped it in his mouth.

Red flooded the man's face and he hunched his shoulders. "Guilty as charged, though I try to keep it under wraps. Still, Rick just got back in town...think they've had something going on long distance?"

Annabelle dropped her gaze to her food. Probably better to simply ignore the conversation. She'd give Ben props for trying to divert Alan's attention. The woman beside Alan chimed in with her thoughts on the subject. And while, yes, Rick was, to use the woman's words, a "handsome specimen," Annabelle couldn't believe he'd had anything going on with Angel long distance. The woman had been throwing herself at

Rick all evening on Saturday, and he'd been deflecting. What had changed his mind? Angel wasn't his type. She frowned. Not that she knew his type. Not anymore. Nor was she even entitled to have an opinion on the matter. She'd had her chance.

And squandered it.

She frowned.

"Something wrong with your food?" Ben leaned over and peered into the green plastic basket that held her tacos.

She poked at it. "No. It's fine. I'm suddenly not very hungry. I think I'll head back to the office and get back to work."

Ben wrapped up what was left of his burrito and stood. "I'll join you."

"You don't have to do that." She took her tray and stepped toward the trash.

"It's fine. When Alan gets on a gossip tear, there's really no stopping him. It gets sticky when you're the HR guy and you start hearing all the ins and outs of employee personal lives. It's better if I avoid it altogether."

Annabelle managed a weak smile. "So it's not always like this?"

Ben shook his head. "Honestly, I forgot Alan was in today. He's usually off site. Sorry about that."

She shrugged. "Seems like there's one in every office. Not having to deal with them is one of the things I love about free-lancing."

He chuckled as she escaped into her office. "Holler if you need anything. I'm just down the hall."

Annabelle nodded and unlocked her machine, her thoughts already drifting to the problem that needed solving. Having the full picture, not the best-case scenario they presented in the request for proposal, necessitated a few changes to her project plan. But she should still easily have it done by the end of February.

"YOU PLANNING ON WORKING ALL NIGHT?"

Annabelle jumped as Ben moseyed into her office and dropped into the guest chair facing her desk. He had his coat over one arm and laptop bag in his hands. Her eyes darted to the clock at the bottom of her screen. Nearly six-thirty. Already? "Lost track of time, I guess."

He shook his head. "I'm surprised you didn't hear everyone packing up an hour ago. They're not exactly quiet."

She shrugged and started saving and checking her code into the version management software. "I get...absorbed. But I'm making good headway, so that's nice. Honestly, left to my own devices, I'd probably keep working another hour or two."

"You really like it, don't you?"

"I do." Programming had always been fun. But in the aftermath of breaking her engagement with Rick and then having her dreams of what life as a software engineer should be shattered, the code had remained constant. Code and God. Not necessarily in that order, though there had certainly been moments when she'd relied more on the software she created than her Creator. Not her finest moments, but there was something to be said for being in control when the rest of your life was adrift at sea.

"Can I walk down to the parking garage with you? Our building's safe—this whole area is, generally—but I don't like the idea of you going down alone. And since you missed the crowd..."

One side of her mouth curved up. He was a considerate man. First lunch, now this. "Were you waiting for me?"

Crimson stole up the sides of his neck. "I had some paperwork to catch up on. Even made a dent in clearing off my table."

"Well. Thanks." She locked her computer and clicked off

her screen. "I think I'm ready. You really don't have to do this though. You know that, right?"

"I know." He stood and slung his laptop bag onto his shoulder. "Do you mind if I say I like talking with you?"

She stopped and studied him. Was he saying he was interested in her? He wasn't Rick—no one was—but he was good-looking in a quiet, understated way. And their conversation on the way to and from lunch had been pleasant. What would it hurt to get to know him? Especially if Rick and Angel were dating. A lance pierced the mended pieces of her broken heart. She buried the pain—a reflex she'd perfected over the last six years. "No. I guess I don't."

He flashed a grin as they walked through the lobby. Speaking of Angel and Rick, there they were, gathering their coats and looking cozy. Annabelle stiffened and deliberately looked away.

Ben pushed open the door and held it while she went through. "Are you doing anything for dinner?"

She had a freezer full of microwavable meals waiting for her at home, plus pajama pants, and at least three hours of work on other projects to get to. She glanced over her shoulder and caught Angel smiling up at Rick. Annabelle turned and met Ben's gaze. "Nothing special. What did you have in mind?"

6

Rick fought the urge to roll his eyes at whatever inanity was coming out of Angel's mouth. Something to do with office gossip. Could she tell he wasn't listening? Out of the corner of his eye, he watched Ben and Annabelle at the elevators, his heart speeding from the simple act of seeing her. She looked less gaunt now, was it simply the light makeup she wore to the office that had been missing at the dinner party or was it something else? Or someone else? Had he heard right? Annabelle and Ben were getting dinner?

Angel frowned. "He works fast."

"What do you mean?" Rick pulled himself back into the conversation. For good or for ill, he'd asked Angel, not Annabelle, out. He owed it to her to be mentally present during their date.

Pink tinged her cheeks. "Ben and I were...not dating, exactly, but headed that way before the holidays. Then the thing with my ex happened and I took a step back. I needed time to figure out what was going on, try and adjust to a new normal, you know? Anyway, I guess I didn't expect him to move on so quickly."

Rick cocked his head to the side. "As opposed to you?"

"Well, yeah. I mean this is really the first date I've been on since then. But if he's asking out the new girl, he's probably already worked his way through any of the other eligible women at IA." She shrugged into her coat and grinned up at him. "I'm ready when you are."

There were so many assumptions in what she'd just said, Where did he even start pointing them out? Probably better not to. If she couldn't see them, it was unlikely having them identified was going to be productive. He tried not to sigh or mentally kick himself for asking her out in the first place. Even if she wasn't Annabelle, she had to have some redeeming qualities didn't she? She was a hard worker. That was one. Did she go to church? He pushed open the door, letting her walk through before pulling it closed and checking to make sure the security locks were on now that it was after hours. The door rattled. People would need their badge to get in. One less thing to worry about after dinner.

He cleared his throat. "Tell me about your church."

Angel's eyebrows shot up. "Um. I don't know that I'd call it my church. I mean, I go there, sometimes. It's...I'm not always...it gets tricky."

"I thought you said you took your daughter?"

"Oh. That church. Yeah, that's where we went when I was still with her dad. All her friends are there and so it's comfortable for her. But since the divorce...it's messy. He still shows up some weeks. Not regularly, but just enough that it's uncomfortable for me. And our friends didn't want to take sides, even though he cheated, so..."

He nodded. He could understand not wanting to go to the same church under those circumstances—he'd spent the rest of his senior semester trying out new churches after Annabelle broke his heart. He hadn't wanted to have to face anyone at their church either—but you still had to get plugged in again somewhere. That had been one of the first things he'd done overseas. And the tiny English-speaking congregation he and Jake both attended was one of the highlights of his week.

After the failure of that conversational gambit, what was he supposed to do? She didn't appear to be bursting with things to talk about. He held open the door to the Pub, nodded when the hostess asked if it was just going to be the two of them, and then did the only thing he was sure would get her talking.

"Why don't you tell me about your daughter?"

RICK STARED at the ceiling and listened to the quiet. How did Gabe handle living so far out of the way? Not that Clifton was rural, but it was this tiny puddle of quaint in the larger suburban sprawl that made up D.C. And yet...there was no traffic noise. His house was surrounded by land—heck, his neighbors actually farmed some of theirs on a small scale. Living near a fairly busy military post in Germany, Rick simply wasn't used to this much silence at night. Throw in Jake for a roommate...it was no wonder that four a.m. was staring him in the face. It was too quiet to sleep. And his brain was too full of Annabelle. He flexed his fingers to keep them from balling into fists. Every time he walked past her office he had to force himself not to look in, to *go* in, sit down, and pour out his heart. And yet, there was no possible way she still felt the same. What was he supposed to do? Work. Work had saved him in the past, it could do it again.

Four a.m. That was...ten...a perfectly respectable time to call. He grabbed his cell off the nightstand and punched Gabe's number. It rang twice before he picked up.

"What on earth are you doing up?"

Rick laughed. "Have you ever noticed how heavy the silence is at your house"

"Not until it was missing. How do you live with Jake without losing your mind?"

"It's an acquired skill. How's everything over there?"

"Running like a well-oiled machine. I didn't need to come."

Rick grinned. He'd tried to tell Gabe that. But it never hurt for all three of them to see how operations were running onsite. "Did Jake manage to hammer out the miscommunication between the Colonel and our billing department?"

Gabe grunted. "Okay, maybe I did need to be here. Jake needs to work on his interpersonal skills a little."

"Yeah. There's that. But it's squared away?"

"Finally. Yes. How're things there? Everything okay? I hadn't actually figured I'd hear from you."

"The office is another one of those well-oiled machines. We seem to be pretty good at making them." His heart...that was another matter.

"I hear a but...?"

"No. Maybe." Rick sighed. "I don't know."

"Hmm. Did you ask Angel out?"

"Yeah, we had dinner tonight. Well, last night."

"And?"

"And...she's still not my type. Her kid sounds neat, though. I kind of let her go on about her daughter once my first conversational salvos crashed and burned. From what I gather, the divorce is as amicable as such things can be. Like they're both actually trying to make it as easy as possible for Chrissy."

"That was my impression, too. Though it was also my impression that Angel and Ben had a thing—or at least the start of a thing—at the end of the year. Obviously not, but still."

"You weren't wrong. She mentioned that. I guess they've both moved on." Rick fought a sigh as he rolled onto his side and switched the phone to his other ear. It wasn't as if he hadn't anticipated Annabelle finding someone else. She was too...amazing? Wonderful? The words didn't do her justice, but they'd have to do at four in the morning.

"Oh? Who's Ben going after now?" Gabe's voice held a hint of resigned amusement.

"Annabelle."

Gabe's exhale crackled in Rick's ear. "Oh."

"Yeah. Pretty much."

"But you're over her. So it's good, right?"

"Right. Of course." Rick frowned as his gut twisted. Six years. How long was it supposed to take for a heart to heal?

"Uh huh. Keep telling yourself that."

"It's that obvious?"

"Not to the casual observer. What are you going to do?"

What *was* he going to do? What could he do? "Take Angel and her daughter skiing on Saturday."

Rick laughed.

"I'm glad I amuse you."

"Sorry."

"No you aren't."

"No, I am. Mostly. How'd you get roped into that?"

Rick shook his head. "I have no idea."

7

"Come on, it'll be fun."

Annabelle shook her head. Who knew Tori could wheedle so well? Though the woman was a reporter...that probably honed your wheedling skills. "I haven't been skiing in...ever. I've never been skiing. My family is more into the beach vacation. The more exclusive and Caribbean, the better."

"All the more reason you should come. You're a grown woman, living on your own, running your own company, for goodness' sake. You should learn to ski. Besides, maybe you'll meet a handsome ski instructor and fall madly in love. That'd fix all your problems."

She couldn't help herself, she snickered. "First of all, this handsome ski instructor is a Christian, right? One with strong beliefs and values that align with mine? And we figure this out...when? When I slip on ice and send us hurtling down the slopes, collecting more and more snow, until we arrive at the bottom looking like a giant snowman, like you see in cartoons? And second, even if that does manage to happen...how does it solve all my problems?"

"I don't remember you being quite this unromantic. Fine, no hot ski instructor. Please come anyway. I really want to go and this weekend is probably one of the last times I'll get to hit the slopes this season. My Dad and his family won't be at the condo, so if we want to spend the night, we could make a weekend of it or, at the very least, soak sore muscles in the hot tub before we leave for home. Plus, I want to spend time with you."

Spend time with her? If she was busy learning to ski, where was Tori going to be? It wasn't as if Tori wanted—or needed—to hang out on the beginner slopes. She took a deep, stabilizing breath, intending to say no. "Yeah, okay."

"You'll come?" Tori very nearly squealed. "This is going to be so much fun! I'll send you an email letting you know what to pack..."

"No. No packing. One day. I have work I need to do this weekend, too. As it is, I'll be up late tonight and tomorrow to try and keep from doing it on Sunday." Annabelle opened a note on her phone and started typing in the to-do list that was rapidly filling her brain. She could get it all done. It'd be tight. But it was doable.

"Spoilsport."

"Hey. I'm going, aren't I?"

"All right, fine. You're sure?"

"Positive. But you can still send me directions to your Dad's condo. It's probably easier to meet there than to try and find each other anywhere else."

Tori cleared her throat. "Do you think we could carpool? My car's making a weird noise and I can't get it in to be looked at 'til Tuesday."

Annabelle frowned. There went her idea of sneaking back home after a few hours. "Yeah, okay. What time should I pick you up?"

"Six?"

"Six. In the morning? That six?" Everything in Annabelle seemed to sink into the floor. Who got up that early to go ski?

Tori's voice held an apology. "It's kind of a long drive out there...and you want a full day on the slopes, right?"

Not really. But Tori apparently did. "Six it is."

"You're the best. I'll text you my address. Can't wait."

Annabelle hit end on her phone and dropped it onto the desk. "Yeah. Can't wait."

"Can't wait for what?" Ben grinned from her doorway. "Sorry, caught the end of your phone call."

"Nothing important. What's up?" Annabelle jiggled her mouse to wake her screen up and maybe give Ben the idea that he needn't linger. At least working from home she only had phone call interruptions to deal with. Why people felt they needed to intrude in person was beyond her. Though, to be fair, Ben didn't do it often.

He crossed the room and sank into her guest chair. "I was wondering if you had plans this weekend?"

She winced and gestured to her cell. "Just made some. I'm going skiing with an old friend from college. Well, you've probably met her. Gabe's fiancée, Tori?"

"Oh, she's great, isn't she? And an incredible skier. You must like the crazy slopes, too."

Crazy slopes? She shook her head. "I haven't actually ever been skiing."

Ben laughed, his mirth dying off as he studied her expression. "You're not joking?"

"Nope."

"Why don't I tag along? I've been skiing since I was tall enough to hook boards to my feet, spent every winter teaching kids on the beginner slopes as soon as I was old enough to get hired. I can teach you, then Tori doesn't have to hang out on hills that will frustrate her, and I get the bonus of spending a day with you."

"I don't know, this was Tori's..."

"I'm sure she'll be fine with it. Why don't you call and ask her? I can pick you up and we can meet her there."

Annabelle keyed in a quick text. "I'll ask..." Her phone buzzed with a response. Annabelle's shoulders sagged but she pasted on a bright smile. "She thinks that's a great idea. I was going to pick her up—her car's in the shop. I can get you on the way?"

Ben leaned forward and pulled a sticky note off the dispenser. He took the pen out of his shirt pocket, clicked it, and, in neat block letters, wrote down an address. "That's me. What time are you leaving?"

She groaned. "I'm supposed to pick Tori up at six. So...five-forty?"

"That'll work." He stood. "Don't look so worried, it's going to be fun."

Sure. She forced a tight smile as he strode from her office. Two days. She checked the time. Well, one and a half, as her Thursday was nearly half over. Maybe she could sprain her ankle between now and then? Better now than on the slopes.

She glanced up as Rick walked past her office. He didn't even look in. Wasn't it natural to look in an open door when you passed it? And yet, he never looked in hers. Her heart ached. Annabelle squeezed her eyes closed and forced down the hurt. She'd been the one to break things off. And there had been good reasons. In hindsight, she saw that they could have found ways to make things work, that Blackburn's dire predictions were overstated, and that she should have trusted her instincts. But at the time...she'd done what she'd felt was right. For both of them.

And look at him now. Successful. Even more handsome, if that was possible. Still fiercely dedicated to God and making a difference for good in the world. Would he be where he was if he'd gotten married just out of college? Would he have been willing to take a job overseas? Would she have supported him? Now...now she absolutely would drop everything and go. But six years ago, she'd had plans of her own. She'd like to think they would have found a reasonable compromise, something that would have allowed both of them to win, but the reality was she didn't know, not for sure. She could only look back and guess.

She sighed. Guessing wasn't giving her answers...or getting this software written.

∼

"SURPRISE!"

Annabelle clutched the door to her apartment and stared at her mom and dad. "What are you doing here?"

"Annabelle, where are your manners? I raised you better than that. Now come on, invite us in. We didn't drive all the way out here to stand in the hall."

Right. But why had they driven out here at all? She pulled the door open wider. "Of course. Sorry. It's good to see you. I was just in the middle of some work...did you eat dinner yet? I could change and we could go out. There are some great places within walking distance."

Her mother shrugged out of her knee-length dress coat, revealing a classic navy pantsuit. Her ivory pearls added just the right touch of class to the otherwise simple outfit. And she probably hadn't even thought twice about putting the ensemble together. Her father came in and glanced around, a frown etched into his features.

"We've eaten. Though if you haven't, your mother and I could get dessert." Walter Elliot grabbed his wife's coat and handed it to Annabelle.

She looked at the living room through the eyes of her parents and shrank. "Will you sit? I'll go get another chair from the office for me. The arm chairs are quite comfortable."

"Honey, where's your sofa?"

Annabelle closed her eyes. "I don't have one yet, Mom."

"Walter..."

Annabelle laid the coat over the kitchen island and hurried into the office for her desk chair before she had to hear whatever it was her mother was going to say. She was a grown woman. It was all right not to have a couch, or seating to entertain. She didn't entertain and that was her choice. She would not be pressured into turning her life upside down to accommodate her parents. Not anymore. She would honor and respect them, love them even.

Jesus, give me patience.

She rolled her desk chair out into the living room and positioned it to form a little triangle with the other two chairs. "Can I make some tea?"

"No, dear, we're fine." Mary smiled and ran her hand over the arm of the chair. Annabelle blessed the salesman at the furniture store for talking her into the leather. Her mother couldn't find fault with that, at least.

"So. What brings you out on a Thursday night? No parties downtown?" She pressed her lips together. That came out snottier than she'd intended.

Her father scoffed. "There were options. We wanted to see you. And since you're too busy to come to us, we figured it was time to come to you. Your building seems nice. Secure."

He was trying. She'd give him points for that. "It's a good area. I know it's sparse in the main room, but the bedrooms—well, I use one for an office—are much nicer. They're where I spend my time."

"What about when you have friends over? I just...is it money? We could..."

"No, Mom. It's not money. I...don't entertain." She'd leave

off the fact that she didn't really have anyone to entertain. Or hadn't, at least, until recently. Now...even if Tori came over, she had two chairs. Or Benick. Though having him over would give considerably more weight to their...could they even call it a relationship? Friendship, certainly. But two dinners and casual lunches each day didn't translate into more. Not yet. Even if they did have quite a bit in common. She liked him. But compared to Rick, there was no comparison. "Sorry. What?"

"I asked why not. Surely with your contracting business it's important to network. You should be having people over." Her mother offered a soft smile. "Didn't you listen at all in your finishing classes?"

"That's not how the software world works, Mom." Thankfully. "It would be inappropriate to do that. And I do network, just at professional functions."

Her mother brightened. "That's good, then. And do you meet young men at these functions?"

She did. Not the way her mother was expecting, but when you worked in an industry that was primarily male, you did tend to run into a lot of men. And even exchange numbers. "I'm not looking for that right now, Mom. And even if I was, I'd look for a boyfriend at church before anything else."

Walter shook his head. "I still don't understand where we went wrong with you. Going to church is fine, but you take things entirely too seriously. Be good, do nice things for people, the golden rule. That's all you need. Anything more gets in the way of good business. Speaking of which, show me where you do this contracting. Let's see what's more important to you than making a name for yourself in the business world."

"I'm—" Annabelle closed her mouth on the explanation. She wasn't going to change her dad's mind. He was never going to understand the shift in her mindset—that it was better to work for herself and take contracts she believed in, with companies she respected, than to chase money at all costs. She stood. "This way."

FIVE IN THE MORNING. On a Saturday. Sometime in the last week —had it really only been a week since Tori called her about the dinner party?—she'd clearly lost her mind. Maybe she could place the blame firmly on Rick's shoulders. Having *him* back in her life was definitely distracting. She'd spent most of last night unraveling a bug in the IA software that, when all was said and done, had been caused by a variable named *rwInterface*. RW. Rick Wentworth. She'd been thinking of "read write" when she named it, but still.

Annabelle dragged herself out of bed, got coffee started into her large travel mug, and headed for the shower. Why did people strap sticks to their feet, go to the top of a mountain, and then slide down? What was fun about that? Maybe today she'd understand—though it was more likely she'd make a colossal fool out of herself and possibly get injured. Friends. She was doing this so she'd have friends. And maybe, possibly, something more in Ben.

He didn't make her heart accelerate like Rick had—still did, for that matter, regardless of how pathetic that was. But he was kind and funny and they had enough in common that conversation wasn't strained or awkward. That counted for something. Maybe it wasn't the consuming passion she'd had in college, but wasn't that part of why she'd been scared and so easily persuaded to change her mind? There was no risk of a relationship with Ben burning away and leaving nothing in its wake. You had to have fire for that. Marrying a friend wasn't settling.

Marrying? Where had she drummed that up? For today, it was better to set a more reasonable goal: don't make a fool out of herself.

Ben was waiting in the small circle outside his apartment building when she pulled in. He raised his travel mug in greeting as he slid into the back seat. "Morning."

"That it is. You don't want to sit in the front?"

He shook his head as he snapped the seatbelt into place. "Nah. Tori's probably better with directions if her dad has a condo at the slopes. And this way, I can snooze without keeping you two from chatting."

"Got it all planned out, don't you?" Annabelle glanced in the rearview mirror and smiled. He hadn't bothered to shave. It gave him a rakish look, as if there was the possibility of something more dangerous than the boy-next-door vibe he usually gave off.

Ben chuckled. "I'll at least wait to take a nap 'til we're on the highway."

"You're awfully chipper for so early in the morning."

"The military will do that for you. Or it'll make you hate mornings. For whatever reason, my brief stint left me an early riser. So I try to embrace it rather than work against it."

Better him than her. Especially after two late nights in a row. Her parent's visit had left her restless. Was she doing the right thing? She believed she was. But what if...no, that was the way to madness. This was where she'd felt God leading her. Still did. Mostly. Though she questioned that some with Rick back in the picture. No. She wasn't thinking about Rick today. Today was for new friends, for Tori and Ben, not for ghosts with no future. No matter how fast they made her heart beat.

She wove through the early Saturday traffic toward Tori's place. Was there never a time when the DC area streets were empty? Ben seemed content to quietly sip his coffee, so she let him. It took all of her concentration to keep her eyes open and drive. Hopefully her coffee would kick in soon.

Tori was also chipper. She slipped into the front seat already chattering away and didn't pause to do more than sip from her travel mug until they were nearly there. Annabelle's ears hurt. And it was possible they were bleeding. She'd have to find a place to check surreptitiously. Thankfully, neither Tori nor Ben had appeared to mind that she gave, at best, short, noncommittal responses during their drive.

"Here we are." Annabelle pulled the car into a parking spot as close to the main ski lodge as she could find. There were already several completely filled rows and the slopes had only been open for twenty minutes.

Tori grinned. "You're going to love this, I just know it. And now that you have a bona fide instructor, it'll be even more fun. I'm going to run over to the condo and get my gear—Dad lets me store it in their unit. I'll meet you outside the lodge?"

Annabelle looked at Ben. "Is that okay?"

"Sure. I'll help her get set up." Ben offered her his elbow. "I'm renting today too—wasn't sure how big your car was. I probably could've made it fit, but overall I'm glad I didn't bother. Come on."

It didn't take long to get boots, skis, and poles and for Ben to show her how gear up. Hugging her skis and poles, Annabelle clomped awkwardly behind Ben as he wormed through the increasing crowd around the lift ticket and rental counters toward the rear exit of the lodge and onto the slopes. When was this going to get fun?

"There you are." Tori waved from the bottom of a short flight of steps. "All set?"

"I guess."

Ben laughed. "Try not to sound so excited, Annabelle, you'll make me think you're looking forward to learning."

"Sorry. It's..." Her eyes caught a flash of color and a shape that had her trailing off. That couldn't be Rick. What were the chances that he'd be here today? He lived in Germany, the slopes here couldn't possibly compare.

"It's?" Tori drew her eyebrows together and looked over her shoulder then back at Annabelle.

"Lost my train of thought." Annabelle pasted on a smile. "Now what?"

Ben pointed to the hill in front of them where kids were stepping up the slope sideways before turning and slowly skidding down to the bottom. "Let's start with that. If you can manage it, we'll give the bunny slope a try."

Tori sighed. "I was afraid of that."

He chuckled. "And that is why I came. Go. Maybe by lunch she'll be feeling up to trying something that won't put you to sleep."

"You sure? I...this was my idea." Tori frowned. "I feel like I'm deserting you, Annabelle."

"I'm sure. Ben said he likes to teach. I'll be fine, go. We'll meet back here at noon?"

Tori checked her watch. "Sounds good. Thanks, Ben."

Annabelle watched Tori stomp into her skis and push off toward the lifts before turning her attention to Ben. "All right. Show me what to do."

"You're sure I'm ready for this?" Annabelle glanced at the green circle on the sign at the head of the trail, her stomach quivering. The hill by the lodge had been fairly easy to conquer and they'd moved on to the tow rope. After that, Ben said he was convinced she was ready for more and, before she could talk him out of it, had her in line for the lift. The ride up had been amazing. What a view. She'd caught another glimpse of Rick's doppelganger—it simply couldn't be him—as they'd passed over an expert slope. That man was skiing with two women—his wife and daughter if her glimpse was accurate—which made it even less likely that it was Rick. Why was she seeing him around every corner? Especially when she was here with Ben, sort of.

"Positive. Worst case, you fall down. But we've gone over getting back up, so..." Ben shrugged.

Right. Easy as all that. "Okay."

"That's the spirit. I'll try to stay close, but you go at a speed that's comfortable for you. Keep your eyes and ears open, and if we get separated, I'll wait for you at the bottom of the hill." He pushed his sunglasses up and, with a bolstering smile, pushed off.

Annabelle took a deep breath, double-checked the chin-strap on her helmet, and followed suit. This trail was busier than the area where the kids were learning. But something about her technique must have screamed "amateur," people gave her a wide berth, calling out clearly what side they were passing on. She went slowly enough that she could lift her head and look around every few seconds instead of staring at her skis. Before long, Ben was out of sight. Her mouth went dry. He'd really left her alone? She snowplowed to a stop and squinted down the hill. It wasn't that steep, or very crowded. She could do this.

Pushing off, Annabelle allowed herself to build up more speed. The wind whipped her face and she grinned. She was doing it. And maybe she understood why people went out of their way to spend a day like this. Soon—too soon—the hill was flattening out. She spotted Ben to the side of the trail. A tiny jolt shook her as their gazes met.

"I knew you'd be great. What'd you think?" Ben reached out an arm to steady her as she slid to a stop beside him.

Annabelle gave him a one-armed hug. "That was amazing. Can we go again?"

He laughed and slipped an arm around her, returning the hug, then left it draped over her shoulders as he checked his watch. "We probably have time before we meet Tori for lunch, if you're willing to risk being a few minutes late?"

The weight from his arm was heavy on her shoulders. There were no fireworks, but it wasn't bad. Maybe the layers she'd worn against the cold kept the tingles to a minimum or maybe...no. It had to be the layers. Not every relationship that lasted was filled with overwhelming physical excitement. She and Ben had a lot in common, and she *liked* him. It had been entirely too long since she met a guy she honestly liked. They could have a calm, steady life together, if she gave him a chance. "I don't think Tori will mind. Besides, I can probably go a little faster this time."

"All right, back to the lifts we go." Ben slid his arm off her shoulder—was that regret in his eyes? Maybe he was thinking the same thing. They were going to have to talk about this—whatever it was—before too much longer.

"Make a path!" A man in a red jacket and black ski pants called out as he hurtled down the intermediate hill they were passing. Behind him, another member of the ski patrol pulled a bright red toboggan with slightly less hurry to their movements. Two other skiers followed close behind, one weeping loudly.

Annabelle stared as the group came nearer. It was the man —Rick's lookalike—and the woman in the sled...her jaw dropped as it was dragged past. That was Angel. Which meant it wasn't Rick's doppelganger, it was Rick.

"That's Angel." Ben frowned and turned his gaze to Annabelle. "Did you know she was coming today?"

Annabelle shook her head.

"Ben? Is that you?" Rick skidded to a stop sending up a spray of snow.

"Rick? What are you—" Ben made a cutting motion with his hands. "Never mind. Was that Angel? What happened?"

"Ben? Oh Ben." The weeping, teenage girl beside Rick

threw herself at Ben, her skis tangling with his as she slumped into his arms, sobbing. "Mom was showing off that trick you did when the three of us came skiing before Christmas. I told her not to. She'd never tried it before. I think she would've made it, but the tip of her ski got caught on something and she went flying."

Annabelle swallowed. That didn't sound good. She looked up at Rick. "Is Angel okay? Did she hit her head?"

Rick scrubbed a hand over his face. "I didn't see her hit her head, but she's dazed and in pain. Her shoulder hit the ground first. Come on, Chrissy, we can follow the ambulance in your mom's car."

"Nooooo." The girl continued to cling to Ben. "Can't you take me, Ben? Please?"

Ben shot Annabelle a helpless look.

Annabelle patted his arm. "Go, Ben. Chrissy needs to be with her mom. Call my cell when you know something."

"Thanks. I'm sorry, Annabelle." Ben eased Chrissy out of his arms. "Let's go find your mom."

Annabelle watched them ski after the patrol, winding through the crowds that were already taking over the cleared space, then turned to Rick. "Shouldn't you go, too?"

"I don't think I'm needed. Or wanted. I'd just be in the way."

"Why don't you come get a cup of coffee with me, then? We'll wait for Tori, who's joining me and Ben—well, me at least —for lunch and wait for Ben to call."

8

Rick laced his fingers together. It was that or fidget with the steaming mug of coffee in front of him, and Annabelle was doing enough of that for both of them. When she wasn't tapping or spinning her cup, she was checking her phone. Even with a part of his mind still on Angel, he couldn't stop the warmth, the rightness, of sitting here with Annabelle.

"Won't it ring or chime or something?"

She jumped, the phone clattering to the table top. "Sorry. Yes, of course it will. I just...why aren't you worried?"

He was. Not, probably, in the way she expected him to be. But when an employee got injured as badly as it had looked, he was concerned. "Who says I'm not?"

She lifted her brows but simply shook her head.

What did that mean? She never used to be one for ambiguous gestures. The fact of the matter was, he couldn't concentrate on Angel with her in front of him. He had to tell her. Maybe it was dumb—it was a risk, certainly—but if he'd gotten anything out of his attempt to date Angel it was that

Annabelle was still the woman he wanted in his life. "Annabelle...I..."

"There you are. Oh, hi Rick. Where's Ben? This place is more crowded than I expected. Did you order yet?" Tori pulled out a chair, a flurry of snowflakes falling off her coat as she unwound her scarf and sat. "Wait. What are you doing here, Rick?"

Annabelle's mouth curved and she curled her hands around her coffee cup. "Ben went to the hospital with Angel and Chrissy. I'm not exactly clear on what happened, but Angel had some kind of accident and the ski patrol pulled her down the mountain on a toboggan. I thought that was only in the movies. She was skiing with Rick today. You didn't know?"

Tori's expression was one of innocence. "Me? How would I know anything like that? Is she okay? What's the deal?"

"I'm waiting for Ben to call me. Figured lunch was probably as good a plan as any to pass the time. And no, we haven't ordered yet." Annabelle looked down at her phone.

Rick cleared his throat. "Why don't I go take care of food for the three of us? The line looks like it's thinned out some."

Tori grinned. "Such a gentleman. I want soup and a sandwich. I'm not picky, overly, but if they have tomato and grilled cheese, I'll be in heaven. And some coffee."

"Annabelle?" He stared at her until she looked up and met his gaze.

"Um. Sure. That's fine."

He angled his head to one side. "You're sure?"

Annabelle frowned. "Why wouldn't I be?"

She'd despised tomato soup for as long as he'd known her. Had, in fact, been prone to verbal rampages whenever anyone mentioned it. He tucked his hands in his pockets and crossed the room to the cafeteria line. There was no way he was bringing her tomato soup. Six years could change a lot, but not something as intensely disliked as that.

Moving through the line, he paused at the soup and considered the options. He turned toward their table and saw Annabelle and Tori huddled with their heads together. Tori kept gesturing wildly. What he wouldn't give to be a fly on the wall. Had she known he'd be here and convinced Annabelle to come on the off chance they'd see each other? It was farfetched. Very. And yet...Gabe and Tori talked. Couple that with the fact that, to his knowledge, Annabelle had never been skiing as a teen and it was suspicious. Maybe she'd taken up the sport in the last six years but...he didn't believe it. Did she know he'd be here? Or had Tori simply roped her into it with no explanation?

He ladled a bowl of tomato soup, along with two bowls of broccoli and cheese before angling past the salad bar to the hot sandwiches. Grilled cheese seemed to be the order of the day, they were churning them out as fast as the cook could slap them together. Figuring there was no harm in it, he added three thick slabs of chocolate cake to his tray before heading to the cashier. When he arrived at the table, Tori snapped her mouth shut and smiled up at him.

"Thanks so much, Rick. What do I owe you?"

"Don't worry about it." He set a bowl and sandwich down in front of Annabelle. "Any word from Ben?"

"They've taken her back for an x-ray, but they seem pretty sure she shattered her right clavicle."

He winced and dipped his spoon into his soup. That was going to take a long time to heal. "Shattered?"

Annabelle nodded. "He said they're already talking surgery, though they have to wait for the swelling to go down, first. So she can probably go home tomorrow with a brace and schedule the operation at a closer hospital."

Tomorrow. Angel was his ride. Looked like he'd be staying in a hotel out here for the night. He'd start looking into that after lunch.

Annabelle tore a piece off her sandwich and dunked it into her soup. "This is good. Thanks, Rick."

His heart raced when she said his name. Was he imagining it, or had her voice softened? Was it possible she had even a memory of the feelings they'd shared? Of course not. He frowned and stirred his soup. She'd been here with Ben. Even if Tori and Gabe were trying to do something ridiculous by arranging some kind of "accidental" meeting, she'd brought along another guy. And he was here with another woman. A woman who was now in the hospital, and whose daughter had preferred that someone other than he accompany them. Chrissy was a nice kid, but she hadn't taken a shine to him at all.

"Are you okay, Rick?" Tori sat back in her seat, studying him. "We could drop you at the hospital if you're worried about Angel."

Annabelle's phone rang, saving him from having to answer. He resumed eating, though he couldn't have said if the flavor was anything of note.

Annabelle sighed and set her phone back down on the table. "It's like they thought. Chrissy is begging Ben to stay and take them home in the morning. Angel won't be able to drive for a while, she needs to keep the arm immobilized. They want to keep her overnight as they're concerned about concussion. Ben asked if we would take you home."

"Me?" Rick set his spoon down and nodded once. Obviously, whatever marginal chance he'd thought there was with Angel—and he wasn't even convinced he wanted there to be one—was now gone. "That would be great. Thank you."

"LEVEL WITH ME, TORI."

Tori buckled her seatbelt and turned. "What?"

Rick shook his head. "You know what."

"No. Not sure I do."

"Did you plan this?"

Tori looked over her shoulder and started backing out of her parking spot. "Plan...Angel breaking her collar-bone? No. Plan Annabelle dumping you off at my place and pleading fatigue and an early morning so I'd feel obligated to offer to take you back to Gabe's? Also no."

"What about happening to be at the same ski slope where I was taking Angel and Chrissy in an attempt to get to know the two of them better?"

She shifted in her seat as pink crawled up her neck. "I might've heard you'd be there from Gabe. But it's a big ski resort. What are the chances we'd actually bump into each other?"

They were slim. And yet, he'd caught a glimpse of Annabelle several times throughout the day. The people on the beginner hills were always in the way. Plus, they were right there, in the middle of everything. If he was honest, he probably would have seen her anyway. He'd been looking for her, though he'd only realized it when he saw her the first time. Angel hadn't noticed, thankfully. But Chrissy had caught him staring once. Was that why she hadn't wanted him to tag along to the hospital? Probably not. They'd just met. Angel and Ben had dated...obviously Chrissy would be more comfortable with him.

"Why?"

Tori eased the car into the flow of traffic on the highway. "Why what?"

"Why did you ask her to go skiing?"

Tori shrugged.

He frowned and drummed his fingers on his knee. "Gabe told you about us in college, didn't he?"

"He might've mentioned it." Her shoulders sagged. "And I might have pried more of the details out of her."

"Then you have to know it was stupid."

Tori's mouth dropped open and she snapped it shut, her teeth clacking together.

Rick turned and looked out the passenger window, his voice barely louder than a whisper. "She broke my heart and it wasn't even a hitch in her stride."

"You're wrong about that."

He scoffed. How well did Tori know Annabelle? Even if they'd been dorm mates in college as Gabe had mentioned, were they friends, really? Tori didn't know what Annabelle still felt. Couldn't know. Annabelle certainly hadn't given him any indication that she'd been hurting. Not when she'd broken their engagement. Not any time over the past week. Though, if he was fair, he hadn't given her many opportunities. He'd stayed as far away from her end of the offices as possible. The trickles of conversation he'd heard said she kept to herself, was at her desk when the earliest of her coworkers arrived, and was still there when even the latest working employees were leaving. She'd gone to lunch with Ben a couple of times, but even those had been short.

She hadn't sought him out even once.

A tiny voice in the back of his mind reminded him that he hadn't sought her out, either.

Rick shook his head, barely noticing as Tori turned onto the quaint main street of Clifton. Had he really thought she would? He'd seen Annabelle's reaction when she showed up on her first day and found him in the middle of planning a date with Angel.

"Will you let me know how Angel is, when you hear from her?" Tori shifted the car into park.

He nodded. "If I do, yes. I'm not expecting she'll call though."

"Why wouldn't she?"

He lifted a shoulder. It was too hard to explain. But he'd seen her looking at Ben. For all her protests that she and Ben hadn't had chemistry, they had something else. Something steadier. And Chrissy clearly adored the man. He and the girl hadn't clicked at all. In fact, she seemed to despise him on sight. Angel had to take that into consideration. He didn't hold it against her. Perhaps, though, she'd done him a favor. She'd shown him that although he could get back out there, and maybe he didn't have to spend the rest of his life alone, no one would ever measure up to what he'd had—and lost—with Annabelle. With that the case, maybe being alone was the better, more fair, choice.

"Just a hunch. Thanks for the ride."

RICK SAT in Gabe's truck and looked at the steady stream of people going through the doors of the massive church building. It had been a long time since he'd attended a church with this many people. The tiny congregation he and Jake had become a part of in Germany was like family. Could you even find the family that brought you in this crowd? Gabe insisted it was worth dealing with the crowds...and though Rick had skipped church last week, he couldn't do that for the whole of his time in the States.

He pushed open the door and got out. Being late would only make it worse. What he wouldn't give to be back in Germany, where he could ask the questions that pummeled his heart and get honest, carefully thought out answers. Of course, if he was in Germany, the questions wouldn't have resurfaced from where he'd buried them in the first place. And maybe that was the problem. He'd buried rather than answered them.

Rick followed the throng through the door and into the

sanctuary. People were still milling around in the aisles. At least he wasn't late. He scooted into the first pew in the back and plopped down on the end, letting his gaze roam over the room. He caught a glimpse of a familiar figure and stopped. Annabelle. What were the odds? With a congregation of almost eight thousand, maybe the chances were a bit higher than average, but to choose the same service? She looked good, even from this distance. And the distance hid the shadows that lurked under her eyes. They'd been there yesterday on the ski slopes. Was it just that she pushed herself too hard, or did their breakup still plague her as it did him? What did it say about him that those shadows made her even more irresistible?

She turned and looked his way. Their gazes locked. Electricity sparked across the room. He smiled.

Annabelle tilted her head, one corner of her mouth lifting, and she held his gaze for the space of two heartbeats before picking up her Bible and purse and walking toward him.

Rick watched as she picked her way through the crowd, neither hurrying not dawdling.

"Rick."

He fought the urge to chuckle. "Annabelle. You're here alone?"

She gave a slight nod.

He stood and stepped into the aisle, his heart hammering in his chest. "Would you care to join me?"

9

J oin him. Every nerve ending seemed to be on fire. He was only trying to be friendly. Extend an olive branch, that sort of thing. "I'd like that."

"Do you attend here? I—Gabe never mentioned it."

"I mostly go online. They stream their services live, or you can watch the recordings. Either way, it's less trouble than dealing with the traffic, and the parking, and all the people." She lifted a shoulder. "Today...I needed the crowd."

He arched a brow.

She chuckled. It was unlike her. Especially after a full day with people yesterday. But skiing had proven to be less social than she'd anticipated. Not that she'd be signing up to go again anytime soon. But at least she hadn't broken any bones. "Have you heard from Angel? Is she okay?"

"I got a text letting me know she'd need to take this week off. Her arm is immobilized while they're waiting for the swelling to go down so they can operate. Driving would be too difficult—plus right now they have her on some pretty heavy medication."

She searched his face. Had Angel's text really been that impersonal? She'd been under the impression that there was considerably more going on than that. From the way Angel had thrown herself at Rick at Gabe's dinner party...the sudden switch didn't make any sense. Or maybe he was leaving that part out. It was, after all, his business. Not hers. "Well, when you see her, tell her I hope she feels better."

"You should just let her know yourself. I doubt very much I'll be seeing her again before I head back to Germany."

"Head back? But I thought—that is, Tori said you were here through February. You're not staying?"

Rick shook his head. "There doesn't seem to be much point. Everything is running so smoothly here. All my work is there. I might stop and see my sister in England on my way, but..."

The smile froze on her face. It wouldn't matter. It couldn't. "That's nice then."

The worship band started in on the first song, effectively cutting off any reply he might have made. Annabelle struggled to focus on the music. How often had they stood next to each other in church on Sundays in college? Her fingers itched to twine with his as they always had. She glanced at him from the side of her eye. If he felt anything, it didn't show.

When they sat, she scooted away, widening the distance between them in an attempt to calm her traitorous heart.

ANNABELLE CHANGED out of her Sunday clothes and stowed them away in the closet before pulling on flannel pajama pants and a long sleeved t-shirt from college. Tugging thick socks over her feet, she went into the office and booted up her computer. She'd finally wrangled permission from Gabe to do some work at home since it was the test data, not the program itself, that was sensitive. She didn't need the data right now. And as much as she tried to avoid working on Sundays, after sitting next to Rick through church—hoping against hope he was going to suggest lunch, only to have him offer a tight smile and stalk off as soon as the final prayer was over—she needed something she understood. And that was code. Code never let you down.

The wallpaper on her monitor mocked her. She'd changed it several times over the last week—had it really only been a week? But she kept coming back to the photo of her and Rick. It was...perfect. The sum of all her hopes and dreams rolled into one moment. Why had she let herself be talked out of marrying him? It wasn't a question of loving him. She'd loved him, just as she loved him now. And how pathetic was that? She scoffed. Six years later and still in love with a man who couldn't even follow through on the idea of a friendly gesture like asking her to sit with him. They'd been friends before they were ever in love, extending their time into lunch would have been a natural way to try and reclaim that, wouldn't it? She'd hoped—prayed— that Rick heard the same things she did this morning when Pastor Brown spoke. She minimized the development window and opened a web browser, typing in Isaiah 43. She scrolled down to verse eighteen and read it again. *A way in the wilderness and streams in the desert.* What a beautiful thought. It was almost as if God was saying there was a way back for the two of them.

And then Rick had charged off before she could say goodbye.

Annabelle sighed and turned her attention back to the section of code that was giving her trouble. She couldn't unravel her love life, but she could at least try to get this project finished. Sooner rather than later.

When her phone rang, she answered and wedged it between her ear and shoulder so she could continue to type.

"Annabelle Elliot."

"You sound so serious."

"Ben?" Her eyes scanned the code, locking on the variable with transposed letters. No wonder it kept crashing.

"Got it in one." He laughed, but it was an awkward sound.

She fixed the statement, double checked the formatting and hit the compile button. "What's wrong?"

"There's no easy way to say this. I—that is, Angel and I—you see, we'd been dating, I thought seriously but she didn't, and then Rick came and then there was the ski trip and Chrissy was so mad, but now...I think everything is coming together. I'm sorry."

Annabelle squeezed her eyes shut and tried to concentrate on the words he was saying. He'd told her about dating Angel...oh. "The two of you are back together."

"Yeah." He sighed. "Are you angry?"

Was she? Not really. Not even disappointed, if she was honest. "Of course not. We weren't an item, Ben."

"I'm really sorry."

"You said that. Don't be."

"I don't want it to be awkward at work."

Now she chuckled. "I'll be gone before you know it. I'm a little ahead of schedule. Honestly, if things keep going this smoothly, I'll be done by the end of the week. Even if there was a reason for it to be weird, which there isn't, there simply won't be time. Thanks for letting me know."

She hung up and scrolled to the bottom of the program where she began typing. Just one more reason to hurry up and complete the project and leave IA, and Rick, behind. The phone rang again almost immediately. Annabelle looked at the display and dropped her head into her hands with a heavy sigh. Just what she needed.

"Hi, Mom."

"Annabelle, how are you? I thought you were going to join us at the Cathedral for services today, we did talk about it."

They had, that part was true. And she'd said it wasn't convenient. "Mom. I thought you understood I said no. What's up?"

"Sunday is Valentine's Day. Your father and I are going to a ball that some of his business friends are hosting at one of the hotels downtown. You simply must come. I insist."

"I don't have—"

"Nonsense." Her mother cut her off. "You can make time. It's one evening. You don't have to stay the whole night, but it will mean a great deal to your father to have you there. I've put the invitation in the mail for you and a guest. We'll see you then."

Annabelle hit 'end' and closed her eyes. *God? I'm not sure what all this is about, but I'd really appreciate some guidance.*

"So I hear you're the world's fastest programmer." Gabe strolled into Annabelle's office on Tuesday afternoon and sat down across from her.

She clicked save and smiled. "I don't know about that, but this is going well. I think I'll be finished by close of business Friday."

His eyebrows winged up. "That's two weeks early."

"Yeah, well. I've been putting in extra hours. The time I'm billing you for will be about the same as what I bid. So you're not getting a deal or anything." Many of those extra hours could be placed completely at the feet of Rick and the insomnia his presence in her life again had caused. But there wasn't really a reason to mention that. Not to Gabe.

He laughed. "Good to know."

She smiled and watched him as he looked around the

office. Was she supposed to start a conversation? He clearly had more he wanted to say. "I take it things in Germany are going well since you're back two weeks earlier than Tori initially said. Even still, I'm surprised you're in today. Didn't you fly in last night?"

"Yeah, but I slept pretty well on the plane. Figured I'd just come in to the office rather than kicking around at home. The fact of the matter is they don't really need us onsite anymore. Not permanently, at least. Maybe a trip here and there, but the climate's changing." He rubbed the back of his neck.

"That'll disappoint Rick. He said he was heading back soon."

"Oh, Rick'll adjust. We'll finally get to develop the full product we've been planning since day one and move into more of a customized solution space for our contracting. This project—your work—is meant to let us dip our toes in the water. See if that's a viable direction."

She'd wondered about that. After talking—even as briefly as she had—to some of the employees, what she was working on hadn't appeared to fit all that well within the type of work they were currently doing. "And your existing staff?"

"Most of them were hired with a long view in mind. And it's not as if the work we're doing from here is going anywhere. It's just the overseas piece."

"Ah." Why was he telling her this? She was just a contractor. A very temporary one, at that.

"So, given that, I was wondering if you'd ever put any thought into hiring on at a company full time. We're going to be looking for someone to head up the product development. From everything I've seen and heard you'd be ideal."

"I..." She shook her head. It was a tempting offer. But Rick...he'd be back in the office once they closed everything down in Germany. She couldn't be around him every day, working with him—surely he'd be in charge at the top level, given his qualifications.

"Don't answer right now. Just pray about it. Okay?" Gabe stood. "And when you have something you can demo, I'd like to have an all-hands for the technical staff and show it off."

Annabelle stared after his retreating form. The jetlag must have gone to his brain.

10

"How'd it go?" Rick looked up from the laptop he was working on at the table in Gabe's office. If he was going to be moving back here, he needed to figure out office space. There was one more reasonably sized office on the other end of their floor, but Jake had called it as soon as he'd heard the news. Perhaps they could share. It was large enough, and they were used to cramped quarters.

Gabe stuffed his hands in his pockets and strode to the window. "Hard to say. I cut her off before she could say no, but she was already shaking her head. Even so, the interest is there, I could see it in her eyes. I suspect her hesitation is personal more than anything."

"I was afraid of that."

Gabe turned, leaning against the sill. "Why haven't you asked her out?"

Rick sighed. A man had his pride, didn't he? "I thought you were telling me to give Angel a chance."

"Nuh-uh. Don't try that tactic. I did say that before I realized you were still every bit in love with Annabelle today as you had to have been six years ago. Maybe even more. Besides, from the look on Benick's face when I asked about Angel, I'd say your chance with her has disappeared." Gabe pulled out a chair and sat. He rested his elbows on the table and clasped his hands. "Talk to me, Rick. I can't help if I don't understand."

"That's just the problem. I'm not sure *I* understand." Rick stood and paced the length of the room. "It's been six years. She broke my heart and yet, she still holds all the pieces. I can't seem to get them back in order to even try to put them back together. How is that possible? When we're in the same room she's cordial, but there's no indication of more, no encouragement. How do I risk approaching her again?"

"Are you willing to live with yourself if you don't?"

GABE'S WORDS echoed in his head for the rest of the day and he was no closer to having an answer. Could he go the rest of his life without Annabelle in it? Dumb question. Obviously he could, he'd been doing it for this long. But was that the life he wanted? Particularly now that he wouldn't be escaping back to Germany where he could pretend that the nature of his work wasn't well suited to marriage.

He needed to look for an apartment. Or a house. Something. He couldn't keep living with Gabe now that he knew he'd be relocating here. And he should see about having his car shipped over. How much was that going to cost? Maybe he'd be better off selling it and buying something new. So many details...and all of them were good distractions from thinking about a life without Annabelle.

"Hey."

Rick looked over at Gabe. "What?"

"Did you hear anything I said?"

Rick shook his head. "Not a word. Sorry. Thinking through the logistics of moving back here. What's up?"

"Tori just called. She's going to be here in a few minutes and wants to grab dinner. You want to join us?"

Which was worse, dinner with a happily engaged couple or alone? "Where?"

"There's a great restaurant in Clarendon, Season's Bounty. We've been a handful of times. All local, seasonal, and organic. But the chef is a whiz—it's not all salads and dirt."

Rick laughed. "Any possibility of a steak?"

"Oh yeah. And you've never had beef so tender."

That was promising. And a better option than any of the drive-thrus on the way back to Gabe's place. "Yeah, okay. You sure Tori won't mind?"

"She told me to invite you."

Rick smiled. Tori was a keeper. She seemed to be really good for Gabe and she was thoughtful. Even if she meddled. He hadn't quite forgiven her for the whole skiing incident, though he could hardly blame her for Angel breaking her collar-bone. Or for Angel and Ben getting back together as a result. In some ways, he ought to thank her. He'd been awfully close to settling for the first woman who showed an interest without any thought to what God had to say on the matter. Not that he'd been doing much praying about his love life. One more thing that needed to change.

"Knock knock. You boys ready?" Tori strolled into the office and kissed Gabe's cheek.

"I am. Rick?"

Rick nodded as he closed the lid of his laptop. He hadn't made any progress on the report he'd been staring at for the last hour. Better to put it all aside and try again in the morning. "Yeah. Let's go."

Since it was a little too chilly to walk the eight blocks from the office, they all piled into Tori's car. The sidewalks were full of braver folks walking home from work or browsing the trendy shopping area. She steered into a garage and found a street-level spot with relative ease. After dashing across the street, they didn't have to wait long before being escorted to a table in the busy restaurant.

"It's Tuesday. Why are so many people eating here?" Rick shook out his napkin and put it in his lap.

"Food's good, like I said." Gabe peered over the top of his menu.

Tori fidgeted with her silverware.

Rick watched her with interest. Gabe's fiancée had never been what he'd have termed the nervous type. He caught her eye. "Something wrong?"

Red flooded her face and she let out a *whoosh* of air. "I guess I should give up my dreams of playing professional poker."

Gabe chuckled. "Surely this isn't news to you?"

She lifted a shoulder. "Not really. Though I thought I was getting better."

"What's up?" Gabe laid his menu on the table.

Tori drained half of the glass of water in front of her. "Church is having a Valentine's Day dinner for the senior adults and they need servers. I really want to help...and I was hoping I could get both of you to volunteer too. It's going to be at five, probably over by seven, so it's not as if we couldn't still go out ourselves. Well, sorry Rick, you're not invited to that part of the evening."

Rick laughed. "Wouldn't go even if I was. But I can help. It's not like I have any plans. Are they doing it on Sunday?"

Tori nodded. "Gabe?"

"If you're helping, I'm helping. I'll see about moving our reservation."

"You made reservations already? I figured I'd have to remind you." Tori winced. "I didn't mean..."

Gabe waved it off. "I know what you meant. But I do, in fact, look at the calendar sometimes."

"Where are we going?"

"Nope. That's for me to know." Gabe turned to Rick. "You're not going to make plans with someone? It seems sad to spend your first Valentine's Day back in the States as a bachelor."

First. Tenth. The number didn't really matter when he was still going to be alone. Best to just get used to it. Besides... "Valentine's Day is a terrible day for first dates."

VALENTINE'S DAY. How had he missed that was just around the corner? While it might be a horrible day for first dates, it was an ideal day to propose. Or so he'd thought. Annabelle had seemed to find it romantic, too. For a few days, at least. Rick cast a glance at the closed door to the bedroom Gabe had given him before crossing to his suitcase and digging down to the bottom until his fingers closed around a small, velvet box.

He carried the box back to the bed and stretched out, flipping open the lid to stare at the emerald-cut diamond that Annabelle had given back with the shattered pieces of his heart. He'd nearly listed it for sale any number of times over the years, but something always held him back. It took no effort to pull up the memory of Annabelle's face, glowing in the moonlight, as he'd knelt on the ground and offered her his future. Just as easy to recall were her tear-streaked cheeks as she'd dropped the ring into his palm and closed his fingers around it, clinging to his hand and begging him to understand.

He snapped the box shut.

Why would God not allow him to forget? To move on? The few times he'd tried had ended up like the most recent debacle with Angel. Wrecked. Usually quickly.

Oh, Annabelle.

Sitting next to her on Sunday had rekindled something in his heart. Hope. But was there really a chance after all this time? The pastor's sermon had hit home as well. Could God be doing a new thing? Would He really make a way in the wilderness of his life? A stream in the desert of his heart? He yearned for it even as he couldn't imagine it being possible without Annabelle back in his life.

Was it possible?

11

"You're a hard woman to get a hold of." Tori checked over her shoulder before sauntering into Annabelle's office and plopping into an empty chair. Annabelle barely looked up before continuing to type. "I've been putting in crazy hours this week. I...just need to get this project done and move on. You know? How'd you get in here?"

"I have an in with one of the owners." Tori knocked on the desk. "Any chance I could have your undivided attention for a minute? I promise I'll get out of your hair quicker."

"Yeah, sorry." Annabelle clicked save and clasped her hands together. "Shoot."

"What are you doing on Sunday afternoon?"

"I don't have firm plans. I'd sort of expected to sleep for as long as possible and then play it by ear. My parents have demanded my attendance at some big to-do in Georgetown in the evening. I still haven't figured out if I'm giving in and going or not. It'd be easier if there was any possibility of taking someone with me. But there isn't, so...as it is, I've been putting in twelve to fifteen hour days trying to finish up this project. I'm nearly done. If all goes well, and unexpected visitors don't take forever, I can actually leave at a reasonable hour today and have a semi-normal weekend."

Tori pressed her lips together and stood, her back stiff. "Sorry to bother you. I'll just go."

Annabelle rubbed her fingers against her eyes and sighed. Where had the snap in her words come from? "Please don't do that. I'm sorry. I'm tired and I'm tense. What's going on Sunday?"

Tori cocked her head to the side. "You sure?"

Annabelle nodded.

Tori grinned. "The senior adults are having a Valentine's Day dinner and need servers. I've been trying to round up people to help. I have a couple—Gabe, Rick, me, maybe a few others, they're still figuring out logistics. But I thought maybe you'd be willing to help, too?"

"Because I couldn't possibly have plans?"

"No, silly. Do you? You just said you didn't. Though I guess you've got your parent's thing. So maybe that's an issue, but we'll be finished at the church before anything fancy would even be starting. Probably." Tori crossed the room and dropped back into the chair.

Annabelle laughed at Tori's frenzied rambling. "No, there's no one. And, like I said, I don't know if I have plans or not. Being commanded to appear by my parents doesn't automatically result in my showing up. I've finally gotten past the need to try and please everyone by giving in to expectations, no matter how persuasively they're stated. Even if sometimes I have to work through a little guilt to stick to my guns." She flashed a grin. "I guess I worried you assumed I *couldn't* have them. I'm...in a mood. I'll apologize again."

"So...Sunday?"

Sleeping all day...wasn't likely to happen. Not in reality. If she was lucky, she'd swing an extra two or three hours. But her body simply wasn't wired for all-day sleeping marathons. No matter how exhausted she was. Doing something useful would help keep her mind off yet another Valentine's Day without Ri —without a date. And even if Rick was going to be there, they'd be busy. If he was moving back to the States—to the D.C. area —she was liable to run into him from time to time. She'd get over it. "What time?"

Tori clapped her hands. "Yay. I'll text you all the details. Next time I call and text you incessantly though? Could you pick up? Please? It's enough to give someone a complex."

Annabelle chuckled and drew an X over her heart. "Promise."

"All right. I'll let you get back to it. If you're bored Saturday though, give me a call. I've been wanting to check out some of the bridal shops and there are a couple having sales...I'd rather not go alone. Maybe you could find the perfect dress to wear to your parent's party."

There wasn't much that sounded worse than a day looking at wedding gowns and party dresses but Annabelle smiled anyway. "I'll let you know."

Tori scoffed. "Which means no. But think about it. Otherwise, I'll see you Sunday." She turned when she got to the door. "If Gabe didn't already have reservations somewhere, I'd ditch him and go to the party with you. Still will, if you need me to."

"Nah. But thanks." Touched, Annabelle watched Tori leave. Should she go to the party? They were her parents. She respected them. Loved them. But if she'd figured anything out in the last six years, it was that she wasn't going to be so easily swayed by what other people thought she ought to do anymore. When no answer immediately came, she ran a hand through her hair before turning her attention back to the final tweaks to the project. It was, essentially, finished. She just needed to put together a self-extracting installation program and make a few corrections to the user guide.

"THAT'S IMPRESSIVE. This is potentially a game changer for us. Well done, Annabelle." Gabe leaned back in his chair and pursed his lips. The team members who had been present for the demo filed out of the conference room, occasionally tossing a compliment her way as they left. When the room was empty, he leaned forward and tented his fingers. "Have you given any more thought to my offer?"

Annabelle closed out of the demo and shook her head. A small group of analysts stood outside the door chatting, but she didn't see Rick among them. She wet her lips. "I'll be honest, it's tempting. But, Gabe? There's no way I can work here day after day with Rick. I don't know how much of our history you know —enough, I imagine. Watching him with Angel nearly killed me. And sure, six years later, I should be over it. I know that. Especially since the breakup was my idea. But...I'm not."

Gabe frowned. "You think Rick has moved on."

"Of course he has. He's been living in Germany, for crying out loud. It isn't as if he's had the time—or inclination—to sit at home and bemoan lost love. He certainly wasted no time asking Angel out. Which is fine, it's his prerogative. It isn't as if I expected him to spend the rest of his life pining for me. Frankly, I didn't expect to spend the rest of my life regretting my decision. But that's the way it's turning out. I can live with that, mostly. But not if I'm around him every day. If I was going to quit freelancing, IA is exactly the kind of place I'd want to work. You've got friendly, capable employees, and you're doing something that matters. Honestly, it'd be ideal if it wasn't for my heart." Her cell phone chimed as several new texts came in. She ignored it and finished packing up her equipment.

"We don't need to hire someone right away. I'll keep the position open for you for a bit. Let me know if you change your mind." Gabe stood and offered his hand. "You really did an incredible job with this project."

"Thanks." Heat suffused her face. Her work was solid, but it wasn't anything extraordinary. Any of the programmers who already worked here could have done it with some guidance. Was that the difference? She hadn't needed someone to hold her hand? That just meant she liked to be independent, didn't it?

Whatever.

Leaving the conference room, she saw Rick tucked in the corner. Probably waiting on Gabe. Would he have been able to hear what she said? Hot lead settled in her stomach. Even if he'd heard, she couldn't do anything about it now. Best not to dwell on it. She carried her laptop and the left over handouts with her back to the office she'd been using. Time to pack up and go—though she hadn't brought anything personal to decorate the space so packing up wouldn't exactly take hours.

Annabelle sighed and dropped into the desk chair. She swiped her phone and frowned. Whose number was that? Probably another mis-text. One corner of her mouth quirked up. Those were usually good for a grin. She tapped the first message.

I have to say something, but I know better than to barge in and make myself heard. I only hope you'll read these texts and understand my heart. You pierce my soul. Can it be true that you still love me? That your feelings for me remain? My heart is still yours, as it was six years ago. I've been foolish, and unkind, but I have never stopped loving you. Gabe mentioned you were helping at the Valentine's party on Sunday. If you truly still love me—if there is a chance for us to try again—a word, a look will be enough. Yours. Always. Rick.

She dropped her phone on the desk as her head fell back against the top of the chair. Could it be? But...he'd given no indication that he'd heard them when she walked past. How could he hide his feelings so well? And how had he heard what she'd said? It wasn't as if her conversation with Gabe had been loud.

It didn't matter. He still loved her! Was that even possible after how she'd treated him? And all the years in between...her eyes closed. She didn't deserve him.

Tori stuck her head in the doorway. "Hey, you're still here."

"Just finishing up. You and Gabe heading out to dinner?"

Tori grinned, nodding. "Friday night."

"If you see Rick, you'll remind him about Sunday? Make sure he's coming and doesn't bail?"

"He said he'd come." Tori frowned. "What's going on?"

Annabelle stuffed her laptop into her bag, checked that everything was turned off, and grabbed her purse. "Has he left? Do you know?"

"Last I saw, he and Gabe were finishing up in Gabe's office. I'm going to ask again, what's going on, Annabelle?"

She smiled and grabbed Tori's hand, giving it a quick squeeze. "I'm not entirely sure, but I think it's good."

"ANNABELLE?"

She looked up, her hand stilling as she fumbled in her bag for the key to her car. He was waiting for her? The breath left her body. "Rick?"

In three long strides, Rick crossed the aisle of the parking garage and slipped his hand into hers. "I tried to forget you. I thought I had."

Laughter bubbled through her as she looked into his eyes. Her nerve endings were on fire, sensation pounding from all directions, though only their fingers touched. "I was wrong, Rick. So wrong. Can you forgive me?"

In answer, he lowered his mouth to hers. The familiar

shape of his lips against hers soothed even as it excited. And more than that, it was like coming home. Awareness of their surroundings returned slowly and she eased back.

"Is that a yes?"

He smiled, letting out a short chuckle. "Yes. Are you free for dinner?"

"Let me check my schedule." She held his gaze with her own and counted silently to ten. "Look at that, I'm free."

With a laugh, he pulled her into a tight hug. "I've missed you. Come on. There's a nice place in Clarendon. Feel like a walk?"

"Sure. Let me put my bag in the trunk." When that was done, her keys, phone, and wallet tucked into an inside pocket of her coat, Annabelle zipped up her jacket and wrapped her scarf around her neck. It hadn't been too chilly this morning when she'd come to work, but with the sun gone, it was probably getting cold enough that she'd be glad for the extra layer. Although...being with Rick again might be enough that she wouldn't notice.

He slipped his fingers through hers as they angled toward the street-level exit. Wind whipped between buildings, stinging her cheeks. She looked up at him through her lashes and her lips curved.

"What?" Rick glanced her way, his own smile answering hers.

"I was just thinking about the sermon on Sunday."

His eyebrows lifted. "That...wasn't anything I was expecting."

Annabelle chuckled. "I spent all of church hoping—praying —that you'd suggest lunch. That maybe we could at least find a way to be friends again. How the pastor talked about finding a way in the wilderness made it seem even more God-ordained. And then you stormed off. So I figured that wasn't going to happen."

"I didn't storm off." He frowned. "I said goodbye and everything."

"No, Rick. You didn't. You were out of your seat with a curt nod and through the door before he finished the final syllable of 'amen.'"

"Hmm. Does it help to know I spent the duration of the sermon thinking the same things? Well, mostly. I pretty much decided God was poking fun, dangling you in front of me, and talking about doing a new thing. This," he squeezed her hand, "seemed impossible. And it broke my heart all over again."

Annabelle leaned her head against his shoulder. "I'm sorry. So sorry. I thought I had to prove myself and I let myself believe the dire predictions that painted you as a misogynist, despite knowing the truth. I was scared."

He stopped and held her gaze. "And now?"

Her heart thundered in her chest. "Life without you is the only thing that scares me now."

12

"Here. Tie this on over your clothes." Tori thrust a red apron at Rick before hurrying back toward the kitchen at the far side of the gymnasium-slash-multi-purpose room.

Rick eyed the apron then shrugged. It'd keep his suit clean. And if everyone was wearing them then no one would look stupid. He donned the apron and reached for the ties when he noticed the front of the thing was decorated. The apron was covered with cartoon hearts.

"Nice apron, Rick." Gabe snickered and punched him in the shoulder as he walked past.

Tori hurried back across the room, weaving through the round tables covered in pink, red, and white crepe paper. "There you are. Here, put this on. Then I need both of you to stand at the main door. They're getting ready to let people in. You escort them to a table, seat the ladies, and give everyone a menu. There's a stack of them by the door. Go."

Rick grinned and nodded at the red cloth in Gabe's hands. "Better do as she said. Wouldn't want you to feel left out."

Gabe sighed and looped it over his head. "I knew it was too good to be true. At least we look ridiculous together. Right?"

"Keep telling yourself that." Rick scanned the sea of tables as pairs of servers positioned themselves beside each one. "Have you seen Annabelle?"

"Tori roped her into this too? Poor kid. She's probably in the kitchen. I tried to go help but got kicked out. Women only, apparently, never mind that some of the world's greatest chefs are men." Gabe frowned.

Annabelle in the kitchen? Unless things had drastically changed since college, they'd be better off with a six-year-old. She was great at toast. Anything beyond that...his stomach clenched in reflex at the memories of choking down her attempts to cook. Surely, she'd improved. Safer, though, not to comment. He reached into the box by the door and grabbed a handful of menus. "Ready?"

Gabe brushed a hand over the cartoon hearts and shook his head. "No, but let's get things going anyway."

Once they found a rhythm, Gabe and Rick had everyone seated with a minimum of fuss. There were more senior adults than he'd realized—or they all brought friends since it was Valentine's Day. The considerably smaller number of men appeared to be enjoying all the extra attention they were getting.

Gabe paused while he was carrying a tray of main courses. "Be careful over by the kitchen door. The older lady in purple is a butt pincher."

Rich laughed and glanced over just in time to see the woman in question take a swipe at the passing behind of another server. "I've been asked for my number by three of the women at the front right table. Two said it was for their grand-daughters, but the third said she wanted it for herself."

Gabe snickered. "Maybe we'll get you a date yet."

Rich shrugged but couldn't deny the warmth that spread

through him. He'd spent all day yesterday with Annabelle—they'd taken the Metro into D.C. and gone to the Zoo, then had dinner nearby. Gabe had been busy with Tori, but Rick had still expected questions. "I think I'm good."

"Don't give up, man. I still think you need to talk to Annabelle. But even if you won't do that, there has to be someone out there for you." Gabe nodded to emphasize his comment before hurrying off.

Rick checked in with his two tables. They needed iced tea refills, but were otherwise doing fine. As he made his way to the drink station, he finally found Annabelle. He detoured and whispered in her ear. "Don't let any of these gentlemen steal you away now that I finally have you back."

She laughed as she turned. "Not possible. Love the apron."

Rick shook his head then frowned. "Where's yours?"

"Apparently only the men have to wear them." Her eyes sparkled with mirth.

"So unfair. We're still on for after?"

She nodded.

He grinned. "I'll find you. I need to get this back to my tables. I think two of the women are part camel."

CRICKETS HOPPED around his stomach as he rolled the last table over to the storage dolly. Cleanup had gone quickly with everyone, even the seniors, pitching in.

"You sure you have a way home? I should've thought about that when you caught a ride with me." Gabe tugged the apron over his head and balled it up.

"I bumped into Annabelle. We're going to some party her parents want her to make an appearance at and then she's going to drive me back to your place."

Gabe's eyebrows lifted. "That's...interesting."

Rick tucked his hands in his pockets, his fingers closing around the velvet box he'd brought with him at the last minute. "I think..."

"Someone dropped this off in the kitchen for you, Rick." Tori hefted a large picnic basket by the handle, her eyes full of questions.

He reached for the handle, his muscles relaxing slightly. Step one of the plan complete. "Thanks. It wasn't in the way, was it?"

"No. But..." Tori glared at Gabe as he took her hand and pulled her toward him.

"Come on, we don't want to be late."

"Gabe, quit it. We're fine and I want to know..."

"Tori." Gabe's voice was quiet and he nudged her shoulder with his. "You can grill him later. Let's go. See ya, man."

Rick gave a brief wave and smiled as Tori continued to fuss while they walked across the gym. Where was Annabelle? There was clanging coming from the kitchen. Maybe she was helping with dishes?

He checked for anything missed during cleanup as he crossed to the kitchen. Rick poked his head through the swinging door and smiled as his gaze landed on Annabelle. She was flipping a huge pot upside down on the drying rack. She wiped her hands on the towel she'd slung over her shoulder and turned, giving a little shriek.

"You scared me."

Rick chuckled. "Sorry. You ready? I think everyone else has left."

"Yeah." Annabelle hung the towel over the handle of the oven and untied the apron that covered the purple cocktail dress she wore. Subtle sparkles caught the light and his breath lodged in his throat. She was a vision. Could she really be back in his life? She hooked the apron to the back of the kitchen door and grabbed her purse off the counter. "We can go out this door, as long as we make sure it latches behind us."

Outside, Rick gave the handle a hard tug to check.

"So. My parents' party?" Annabelle fidgeted with her purse. Was she nervous? Rick set the hamper down and gathered her into his arms. He pressed his lips to hers, breathing in the mixture of apple and lemon that was quintessentially Annabelle.

"Better?"

"Than what?" She blinked and looped her arms around his waist.

"Being nervous."

She chuckled. "Got me. Yeah. A lot better. But I'm still not excited about this. I was hoping you'd talk me out of it."

"We'll go, make the rounds, then leave. Promise. Want me to drive?" Rick held out his hand.

She studied him for a long moment before reaching into her purse and handing him the key.

"Mom, Dad, you remember Rick?" Annabelle inched closer, the smile on her face betraying her nerves.

Rick kept his arm around her waist and extended his hand. "It's a pleasure to see you again Mr. and Mrs. Elliot."

Mary's eyebrows drew together as she peered at her daughter. "I thought you said you didn't have a young man. I've been talking with several of my friends all this week—there are people here to meet you."

"Oh, Mom. I specifically asked you not to do that. What if I hadn't come?"

"Of course you were coming. I invited you, didn't I?" Mary shook her head. "Come along, I'll take you around for a few minutes. Rick can stay with your father."

"No, Mom. I—"

Rick gave her a quick squeeze before releasing her. "It's all right, Annabelle."

"She hasn't mentioned you in years. What is it you do again, Rick?" Walter pinned him with a gaze that bordered on predatory.

Rick tucked his hands in his pockets, his fingers curling around the ring box. "I'm one of the co-founders of Intelligence Associates, Inc. You've probably heard of us, we're a solid company with strong family values doing good work to support the military here and overseas."

"Hmm. Seem to recall reading something about another of your founders in the paper not long ago."

"Yes, sir. Gabe runs an annual fundraiser for Operation Mistletoe, it got a little notice this year." That was a bit of an understatement, but when you dealt with a man accustomed to the rich and powerful, it never hurt to downplay things.

"That's right. And you've been living overseas?"

Rick's lips curved. The man was crafty, skirting around the questions he wanted to ask. "Yes, sir. Germany. Though that part of our business is tapering off now, it seems, so I'll be moving back to the area permanently as soon as I can make the arrangements."

"How'd you reconnect with Annabelle?"

Did her father really not know she'd been working on a contract for IA? "She's friends with Gabe's fiancée, so we'd crossed paths. Then, it turned out we needed someone at the office with her considerable programming skills. We were fortunate she was able to work us into her schedule. Your daughter has an amazing talent."

Walter simply nodded, his gaze never wavering.

Rick glanced around the room. Mary and Annabelle were at the far end where tables and chairs had been set up for those who didn't care to dance or mingle. Annabelle looked up and met his look. It was still a jolt to his system. Was it that she couldn't hide her feelings for him anymore, or simply didn't care to bother? Either way, it was heady. He turned back to Walter. "Sir. Six years ago, you and I had a conversation about Annabelle's future. I'd like to readdress it."

"Oh?"

Rick nodded. "Your daughter and I have made some missteps. But she's back in my life. I place that firmly at God's feet and am thankful for it. Later tonight, I'm going to ask her to marry me. I'd like to do it with your blessing."

"You want to marry Annabelle?" Walter turned in the direction of his wife and daughter. "She doesn't seem to be interested in any of the men my wife is throwing at her. You'll have your work cut out for you, you realize that?"

Rick smiled. "I do. But then, so will she. No marriage is without work. I've loved her for nearly ten years. Six of them without her in my life. Now that she's back, I don't want to waste a moment."

Walter extended his hand and Rick shook it. "Good luck, my boy."

He didn't need luck, he had God. For the first time in too long, Rick was full of the surpassing peace that came only from being firmly planted in the middle of God's will.

RICK PARKED in front of Gabe's house and cut off the engine. They hadn't spent long at the party, just over two hours when you included travel time. But it was still creeping closer to nine at night and the thin moonlight left the cold hanging in the air. "Here we are."

"Gabe's?"

"I've spent a little time wandering in his yard since I've been here. If you can even call it a yard when it's this big. Did you know he has a greenhouse?"

Annabelle's eyes widened. "Really? I never would've pegged him as a gardener."

Rick chuckled. "I don't think he is, but you know I've always enjoyed puttering. He said I could do whatever I wanted. Want to come see?"

When she nodded, he pushed open the car door and retrieved the picnic hamper from the trunk. He took her hand. "This way. There are solar lights along the gravel paths—I think those are left over from his Christmas display—so we shouldn't have any trouble."

Annabelle was silent as they walked. What was she thinking? Was this too much too soon? Hopefully not. He was ready to start their life together—the life they should've started six years ago. What would that have looked like? He shook his head. No point trying to figure it out. It wasn't as if they could travel back in time and change anything.

"Here we are." He pulled the door open and gestured for her to enter, smiling at her quiet intake of breath.

"You did all this? It's...amazing." Annabelle dropped his hand and leaned over a riotous display of orchids, breathing deeply before moving to a bed spilling over with lavender flowers. He'd done it for her. It hadn't started out that way. At first it was something to do when he couldn't force his mind to focus on work—an hour here, an hour there. When he'd realized all the plants he was choosing were her favorites, he surrendered to it. The greenhouse had become the one place where he didn't have to deny how much he still loved Annabelle. Even though he hadn't had much free time, he'd made a decent start.

While she moved from one planted area to another, Rick set the picnic basket down and opened the lid. He drew out a red and white checked cloth and spread it over the top of the small patio table he'd found wedged at the back of Gabe's garage earlier that morning. The two folding chairs were ugly, but they were sturdy enough to hold someone. What the setup lacked in elegance, it made up for in privacy.

"There's so much potential in here. I love where you're going with it...it's like a little oasis of spring." Annabelle kissed his cheek before sitting in the chair he pulled out for her. "And it's the perfect place for a picnic. Did you try anything off the trays they were passing? I'd planned to go home and nuke a burrito. This is better."

"I hoped you wouldn't mind. The chance of getting a reservation somewhere was slim. Even the hamper was a stretch...I threw myself on the mercy of the chef at Season's Bounty. Thankfully, she's a bit of a romantic." Rick took her face in his hands and lowered his mouth to hers. He'd meant the kiss to be simple, friendly even, but it turned into something deeper. He wanted more. Grabbing hold of his self-control, he eased back and began unpacking dinner from the hamper. "Do you want to eat in courses, like she suggested, or just open everything up and see what we have?"

"It's late and I'm starved. Let's live dangerously and mix it all up." Annabelle reached for a container and pried off the lid, releasing amazing smells to mix with the steamy earthiness of the greenhouse.

Rick laughed and, after sitting next to her at the table, followed suit. The ring box dug into his leg as he shifted, reaching for each container. He watched as she ate. Did she have any idea how beautiful she was?

Annabelle paused in the middle of the story she was telling about a previous contract and wiped the corners of her mouth. "Do I have something on my face?"

"No. You're beautiful. I've brought up the memory of you so many times. But they were shadows compared to the reality of having you back in my life."

Pink spread across her cheeks. "Rick. You know I don't need flattery."

"It's not flattery when it's true. I love you, Annabelle." His stomach clenched. They'd avoided the words since Friday, almost as if they were each still picking their way through a minefield of doubt sown over the last several years.

"I love you, too." She leaned forward and pressed her lips to his. "Do you remember the photo they took of us walking on campus? They were going to run it in the paper, but never did?"

He nodded. He'd badgered the photographer until he'd sent the file. He'd made a print and had it folded in his wallet.

"It's been the wallpaper on my computer since graduation." She looked down and laced her fingers together. "That probably sounds stupid. Or worse. Pathetic? Stalkerish?"

"It doesn't. I have a copy, too." Rick reached into his back pocket and pulled his wallet free. He slipped the creased and bent photo from its place and held it out.

Everything about her brightened and her face glowed as she took the photo and looked at it. "I wish..."

He put a finger to her lips and covered her hands with his. "Don't waste wishes on things we can't change. We don't know what life would have been if we'd married right out of college. But here, today, as the people we've become, it's enough to know that God brought us back together and gave us a second chance."

She nodded blinked back tears. "I still can't help thinking I wasted a lot of years."

Rick lifted her hand to his lips and brushed a kiss across her knuckles while, with his other hand, he reached into his pocket to draw out the small black box. He flipped open the lid and held it out. "Let's not waste any more. Six years ago, you gave this ring back to me. But it, and my heart, have always belonged to you. Will you take it, and me? Be my Valentine, tonight and forever?"

Tears streamed down her cheeks as her quivering hand reached for the box. "You kept it all these years? Yes, I'll marry you. There's never been anyone else who suited me like you do."

Rick took the ring out of the box and slipped it on her finger. It fit just as perfectly as it had before and sparkled as if it, too, was happy to finally be home. "Can we do it soon? I can't live with Gabe forever."

She laughed and wiped her cheeks. "I'm okay with that idea. You can help me finally buy a couch."

"You don't have a sofa?"

Annabelle shook her head. "I knew once I bought one, I was committing to sitting on it with someone down the road. And since I could never form that picture in my head without you in it, I never bothered."

Rick chuckled. "Is it any wonder I couldn't stop loving you? I'll help you find a couch, Annabelle, and I promise to spend lots of time relaxing on it with you in the years to come."

A NOTE FROM ELIZABETH...

Annabelle and Rick finally found their way back to each other. I think they're going to find the most comfortable couch out there. Don't you?

Cupid's working his way through the team at Intelligence Associates - and now it's Jake's turn. He thinks he's heading into the mountains for some relaxation and a chance to use his professional fireworks license. He's not counting on a single mom and ghosts from his past.

Read Operation Fireworks today to uncover Jake's secrets.

AUTHOR'S NOTE

Thank you for reading *Operation Valentine!* I hope that you enjoyed it! I would appreciate it if you'd help others enjoy it too by leaving a review. Word of mouth is how most people say they find new books to read, so I'd love it if you'd also consider telling your friends about it. Any success my books have is owed to readers like you who take the time to tell others about my stories. Thank you, from the bottom of my heart.

I'm planning two more novellas in the Operation Romance series. Both are planned to release in 2016, so the gang at Intelligence Associates isn't disappearing yet. You can always keep up to date with my writing news via my occasional newsletter. There's a sign-up form at my website (www.ElizabethMaddrey.com) and also on my author Facebook page (www.Facebook.com/ElizabethMaddrey).

I continue to owe a huge debt of gratitude to my husband and sons for giving me the time to write, my sister for her unflinching support and encouragement, and my critique partners Heather Gray and Jan Elder for catching all the times I use the same word six times in two paragraphs.

More than anything, I'm grateful that God continues to give me words and makes it possible for me to write them down.

I'd love to hear from you! You can connect with me on Facebook my webpage or via email.

WANT A FREE BOOK?

If you enjoyed this book and would like to read another of my books for free, you can get a free e-book simply by signing up for my newsletter on my website.

OTHER BOOKS BY ELIZABETH MADDREY

Beachfront Billionaires

Second Chance at the Seaside

Married at the Marina

Billionaire Next Door

The Billionaire's Nanny

The Billionaire's Best Friend

The Billionaire's Secret Crush

The Billionaire's Backup

The Billionaire's Teacher

The Billionaire's Wife

Postcards, A Novel

So You Want to Be a Billionaire

So You Want a Second Chance

So You Love to Hate Your Boss

So You Love Your Best Friend's Sister

So You Have My Secret Baby

So You Need a Fake Relationship

So You Forgot You Love Me

Hope Ranch Series

Hope for Christmas

Hope for Tomorrow

Hope for Love

Hope for Freedom

Hope for Family

Hope at Last

Peacock Hill Romance Series

A Heart Restored

A Heart Reclaimed

A Heart Realigned

A Heart Redirected

A Heart Rearranged

A Heart Reconsidered

Arcadia Valley Romance – Baxter Family Bakery Series

Loaves & Wishes

Muffins & Moonbeams

Cookies & Candlelight

Donuts & Daydreams

The 'Operation Romance' Series

Operation Mistletoe

Operation Valentine

Operation Fireworks

Operation Back-to-School

The 'Taste of Romance' Series

A Splash of Substance

A Pinch of Promise

A Dash of Daring

A Handful of Hope

A Tidbit of Trust

For the most recent listing of all my books, please visit my website.

ABOUT THE AUTHOR

USA Today bestselling author Elizabeth Maddrey is a semi-reformed computer geek and homeschooling mother of two who lives in the suburbs of Washington D.C. When she isn't writing, Elizabeth is a voracious consumer of books. She loves to write about Christians who struggle through their lives, dealing with sin and receiving God's grace on their way to their own romantic happily ever after.

facebook.com/ElizabethMaddrey

instagram.com/ElizabethMaddrey

amazon.com/Elizabeth-Maddrey/e/B00A11QGME

bookbub.com/authors/elizabeth-maddrey

youtube.com/@ElizabethMaddreyAuthor